Bound in the **B**ones

A Donovan's Twist Novella

Maggie Secara

Los Angeles

Popinjay Press

Bound in the Bones

Copyright © 2017 by Maggie Secara

ISBN 978-0-9818401-8-5

Please visit Maggie's website at http://www.maggiesecara.com.

Chat with Maggie and the gang on Facebook at
https://www.facebook.com/groups/maggiesworlds/

Books by Maggie Secara

THE HARPER ERRANT SERIES

The Dragon Ring
King's Raven
The Mermaid Stair

THE RAVEN AT RANDOM SERIES

Black Dog, Grey Lady

ROMANTIC ADVENTURE

Molly September

HISTORY

A Compendium of Common Knowledge 1558-1603:
Elizabethan Commonplaces for Writers, Actors, & Re-enactors

for Nan Earnheart

and about time, too

Author's Note

THE PROLOGUE TO THIS STORY is the Victorian section of *King's Raven*, the second of the Harper Errant novels, where we first met the really quite ordinary Miss Susan Pickering, her rather more dramatic lodger Mr Edward "Ned" Donovan, and the faery sketchbook. They have been insisting on a story of their own for quite awhile now, and here it is. I expect there will be more.

If you are meeting them here for the first time, you may wish to read *King's Raven* first, but is not essential. The peripatetic reporter and the prim spinster share a certain affection, which she has been trying to resist since Christmas, and also a gift. Both can, in the words of the King's Raven of Faerie, hear the bells of Elfland, see things most ordinary mortals cannot.

Those events took place in December of 1854. The new year has past, the summer of 1855 has come to south London, and something is stirring at the house in Albany Road.

Bound in the Bones

I
Incident

MISS SUSAN PICKERING SAT PROPPED up on pillows in her narrow spinster's bed with an enchanted sketchbook on her knees stealing hours from the night in a prodigal expense of lamp oil. Lightly gripped in the rebellious left hand, her pencil skated across the paper.

At the tip of her straight unremarkable nose perched a pair of round steel spectacles. Idly Susan shoved them back into place then returned to the page. Lines flowed, shadows grew, dimension grew so quickly she barely saw the figures in her mind before they had appeared, fully formed. By the time her hand lifted, she felt flushed and her heart was racing. She had covered two large pages with exquisite drawings she scarcely understood. Squinting, she pushed her glasses up again, scrutinized the work.

Each sketch was a story, that much she could tell. Here was a cat curled in a sewing basket, perched on a table where a lady mouse in spectacles was embroidering a sampler. Susan suspected the mouse was herself as she used to be, but what was the cat?

Next was an ornate bird cage housing a parrot in a monocle and Turkish smoking cap.

Along the bottom edge a procession of wimpled nuns glided through a cloister, each figure crisp as a daguerreotype. Were they set in motion, she thought, the nun at the end there would turn and glare at her for using her left hand.

It was worth noting that none of the images had so far stirred to the semblance of life. Worth noting because it had happened before, but then there had been immediate danger to the faery gentleman whose gift the enchantment had been.[1] No danger loomed now, as far as she knew.

The pencil moved again in her hand, the wicked left hand, as her nurse used to say. Even now, long out of the nursery, guilt tugged at her for being so contrary. Moreover, she worked the sketchbook back to front as if it were in Hebrew, or a thing out of Faerie, which in a way it was.

The pictures that swarmed over the page seemed only partly her own, as swift as automatic writing. Drawn from memory, perhaps, or a dream—but not her own. She would have to discuss it with Donovan when he returned.

At his name, a modest smile pleated the corners of her eyes to light the face she knew was plain, but which Donovan claimed to admire.

A fresh page turned under her hand. She could draw him in the dark—the merry eyes, the mocking mouth, the outrageous whiskers that framed his face under that ridiculous bowler hat. No prince of Faerie or of anywhere in the world, just a man. The pencil glided across the paper guided by no other magic than her private affection. Curious, she thought, how brash, ridiculous, transforming Edward Donovan had come into her life at the same time as the faeries, and he could see them just as well as she. Well, he was Irish, of course.

Whilst sharing an adventure at Christmas, he had persuaded her they should address each other by their familiar names, as friends, when they were in private. As a spinster of six-and-twenty, however, and even though he had proposed honorable marriage

---

[1] *Donovan and Miss Pickering's first adventures, and the magicking of the sketchbook, are recounted in the novel, King's Raven, written by Maggie Secara and published by the Poniiav Press in 2017. King's Raven is the second of the Harper Errant series which began with The Dragon Ring.*

half a dozen times since then, Susan found it difficult to comply. She had settled on Edward, his Christian name, for daily use rather than the too-familiar Ned. Or simply Donovan. It helped to retain the barrier that must stand between them. The barrier that was becoming progressively harder to maintain, though she had never told him why.

Where are you tonight, she wondered, shading the planes of his cheekbones, the star at the corner of his mouth. How far from home?

A salaried reporter for the *Illustrated London News*, he had been away for weeks chasing a story as far as Istanbul, by his last postmark. Then yesterday at breakfast, the clipped cadence of a telegram sent from the railway station in Paris: ALMOST HOME. CASE CLOSED. SHARPEN YOUR PENCILS.

That made her smile. Over the next few days, she knew, the reporter would share his adventures as he wrote them up. Susan would capture the details from his words alone, instinctively creating remarkably precise illustrations of places and events she had never seen, for which Ned's editor would pay her a shilling each. She had sharpened her pencils, and the sketchbook had called to her.

The night was warm but she was warmer, restless, even as she lingered over his image on the page. A few more strokes to add a collar, the shoulders of his coat.

"Let's have him on the train," she thought, imagining a rolling English landscape in the carriage window. Or no! Just pulling in to the platform, where she wished him to be.

Finally, pencil thrust behind her ear, Susan sat back frowning at the work. She flipped the pages: the cat, the monks, the bird, and the rest. She started again, even going back to the strange pages from the first time, from last Christmas—those had blurred and faded now, but she examined them anyway, even in the corners. On the next pass, she whipped the spectacles off her face and brought the sketch pad almost to her nose. This curve, that angle, even the random half-lines and false starts and finally Donovan again. The energy leashed within the images made her hands tingle in a way she remembered.

Slowly, Susan put her glasses back on, laid smooth the picture, and settled back into her pillows.

"Show me," she whispered.

Nothing happened, not at once. Then with aching slowness the pencil lines began to shift on their own. Unaided, no trick of light or imagination, the patterns of cross-hatch and shadow created an illusion of depth and movement like the flickering figures in a zoetrope machine, only infinitely more complex and more detailed.

She had drawn Ned Donovan sitting at his ease in a crowded third-class carriage. Now the train halted, billowing steam that obscured him for a moment. Now he stood, set his hand on the latch. He stepped down from the car with his battered old carpet bag in one hand, a fine walking stick in the other, a gift from his editor after the Christmas incident. It was particularly flash, that stick, and must have cost the earth, but the wood was from Africa and exceptionally heavy. In his big hand it swung jauntily as he walked out on the platform. Laughter creased his generous mouth, lifted the ruddy cheeks. He might be recalling a joke, some wild story he would tell her tomorrow or the day after, when he truly arrived—for surely he was in England already. The sketchbook couldn't magic him all the way from Paris, could it?

When he looked up, his glance crossed Susan's and the eyes widened, almost as if he could see her, though surely that was impossible. It was only a drawing, a bit of graphite, barely a sketch. Probably. Still, she smiled back. It was real enough for now.

Abruptly, Ned stopped walking. His graphite brows drew down in doubt, the lines of the mouth compressed. The head tilted as if to catch a curious noise: a voice, his name. The magic in the book rotated his face by stages to look back over his shoulder at something Susan was sure she had not put there.

Only a dot at first, no more. A bit of over-sharpened pencil tip had flaked off under an enthusiastic pen-knife, and lodged in the paper's fibers. Not wishing to smudge, she blew across it sharp and quick. Now there were two dots, or four, and all of them turning in lazy circles. The circles grew agitated, throwing off loops like comets round the sun. They picked up speed.

Before long, three loops had become nine knotted together, then too many to count. They had become a small but energetic tangle of grey wires tumbling toward her. That's ridiculous. Nothing could come off the page. Besides, it was no bigger than the nail of her smallest finger. What harm?

It looked small, she realized, because it was far away, but it was approaching swiftly; she could feel the speed of its coming, its urgency. It was seeking something. It had found Ned Donovan, and he was just standing there, staring at it with interest. In a moment he would take try to bat it away.

She wanted to shout, "No, no. Donovan, walk away! Run!"

Too sensible for panic, she scolded herself instead. Don't be a child. No need to wake the house. It's just a drawing.

Even if she raised her voice he would not hear her. But the drawings in the sketchbook book had reflected real events before. She could almost hear him muttering under his breath, the creak of the wooden platform under his boots. And the thing, too: Susan imagined the hiss and crackle of fire crackers. was that what made him turn around? Did he hear that, or smell the tang of black powder sharp in his nose as it was in hers?

Susan set her jaw into the grim expression that all her lodgers and most of the local tradesmen knew well; the one that made Ned say under his breath: "Though she be but little she was fierce." She had made this thing, or called it forth, so she must have some control over it!

"What good is magic if I can't . . ." She grasped the book in both hands and shook it, hard.

When she looked again she growled in frustration. Nothing had changed, except the chaotic thing had grown, or closed the distance. It was a busy bundle of fluttering ribbons and thick cables governed by a dense cluster at its center. It hurt her eyes to look at it; her stomach rolled.

"Help," she thought, "I should get help."

The fae lord had promised to come if she called, and his folk could not lie, so they said. She had his ring on a thread around her neck. All she had to do was run across the lane in her nightdress and call into the faerie wood.

No time. There was no time.

Blood hissed in her ears, heart thudding under her breast. Her pulse like her mind was already racing. It was only a picture!

She cried out, "Ned, you ridiculous man, run!"

He would not.

It was close enough now she could sees streams of sparks spilling from it, smoky rivers of stars being born and dying. She could almost hear the crackling pops and snaps. With one more burst it swarmed onto the platform where Ned Donovan squared his shoulders; he had held off trades unionists in Durham and rebels at home, and once even vanquished a sorceress. If he was afraid, he hid it well.

In another world, the one where Susan sat clutching the edges of her sketchbook, the balmy airs of summer had become a desert wind, a sirocco drawing all joy and hope from the air. The monstrous thing was no more than the width of her thumb on the page, it must be a hundred times that in whatever reality it occupied. To Donovan it must be vibrating, humming with danger and death. He had no more idea than she of what it was, but no matter; he would face it. Steeling himself, he hefted the powerful walking stick. It rose in his hand.

Susan cried out, "Stop!"

The picture froze.

A gum eraser flew into the plain, unremarkable fingers. It dashed against the tangled knot immobile on the page, scrubbing until only a faint blur smudged the creamy paper. From the table where the oil lamp flickers, she snatched up a new pencil, sanded clean, and pinched away any cinders at its tip.

"I can change this. It can be changed." If she could control her emotions, the magic would be her tool.

Wielding the pencil like a hazel wand, she focused her will. It scratched across the paper with the sound of a skater on ice, hissing and singing as she reshaped the world around Donovan's image. Broad strokes adjusted the scene; a sweep of her thumb added shadow and substance to the platform she knew so well. No longer some anonymous railway station, her crisp lettering named it CRYSTAL PALACE STATION, a chocolate box confection of iron and glass only half a mile away. If he were there, truly there, he was nearly home. She could make him be home.

It was not enough, not quite. Susan could feel the surge of obstructed fury even in erasure.

"We'll have none of that," she said sternly.

A few quick lines suggested luggage balanced on a cart: a much-travelled steamer trunk, a pile of hat boxes barely clearing a hanging basket filled with flowers, transformed out of a few faded loops. Instead of tumbling sparks, trailing blossoms streamed down the sides.

There. That had done it. With the last colorless lines repurposed, the dark energy was silenced, chaos re-ordered. She would have peace tonight, only peace and gentle dreams.

Calmly she commanded: "Show me now."

The drawing moved again when she asked it to. Ned's lifted walking stick that might have become a weapon hailed a hansom cab; the horse trotted smartly out, cab wheels spinning. It made good time through Upper Norwood, turned into Albany Road and trotted crisply past the faerie wood behind its iron gate, bringing him to her door.

Shadows flooded the room as her oil lamp untrimmed guttered out, and with it, the animation. Still trembling, Susan folded away the sketchbook, settled her hands, and closed her eyes.

At last, the bright rattle of a key charged the front door. Lace curtains breathed out and in as it opened and closed. Muffled footsteps on the stair caught on the raveled carpet to make Ned Donovan curse, very mildly; the creaks couldn't be avoided, though he tried.

Old houses are noisy places, full of expectation, as well as creaks, and whispers. In a listening pause, the pulse of relief across Susan's heart was the caress of the Irishman's smile as he hesitated outside her bedchamber. Safe home, he touched his fingers to his lips and then to her door, and passed softly on his way to bed.

As if in response, the once fine house shuddered at its roots. A wave rushed through the rooms and out into the grounds, across the lawns, the gardens and neglected orchard. It swept through the abandoned carriage house, swirled about the tumbled fountain. And something woke.

II
Query

LIKE MANY OF THE LARGER HOMES in the district, Miss Pickering's inheritance had seen better days—most of them before she was born. Its many rooms were capacious and afflicted with rising damp, the ceilings high and crumbling. After several years of economy and careful planning, ceilings patched, plumbing managed, it had become a comfortable, slightly shabby but clean and respectable boarding house.

She had filled it with a small handful of suitable lodgers, a pair of maids, and a boy for general work. Mrs Nixon, the sharp-nosed cook from the depths of Ayrshire, kept them plainly but thoroughly fed. To all of them, the lengthening days meant more hours available for work and fewer hours of uneasy sleep.

So it was that at about ten o'clock on a night in June, by the steady light of a double-globe oil lamp, Miss Susan Pickering sat at the desk in her room and frowned at her sketchbook. She had meant to tidy up some of her views of the Crystal Palace before sending them to a printer that Donovan knew. The printer would strike a few copies and sell them as a kind of *carte de visite*. More than that, he would actually pay her for the originals! That was magic enough for Susan Pickering.

But something had changed. Across the decent stock of the page, the light had dimmed. Blinking, she rubbed at her spectacles with a linen handkerchief, and put them back on. It was happening again. By some uncomfortable, unwelcome magic another goggle-eyed nightmare had begun to take shape under her pencil.

"No!" she whispered harshly. "Stop it."

This time she attacked it with a thick slab of colored wax, blacking it out until the figure blurred and became part of a passing cloud, and she could safely slam the cover on it. She could redraw the image; she would not let that happen again.

Shivering, she set the book aside, resolving firmly to go round to the stationer's the next day and pick out a new one: an ordinary, predictable sketchbook with no theatrics. And with that thought settling her mind, she turned down the desk lamp, folded her spectacles, and went to her solitary bed.

Minutes later, someone screamed. A long wobbling wail declined into a whimper. Into the silence, a low laughter.

"What on earth?"

Annoyed as much as startled, Susan found the lucifers at her bedside, lit the candle, and listened, sparing a glance at the sketchbook. But that was nonsense. The drawings when they moved were frightening, but they made no sound. What had caused it, then?

She let her breath go, deciding that sound must surely have been no more than her over-stimulated imagination. She leaned over the candle flame to blow it out, then a girl's voice lifted weakly.

"No! Don't!"

Another shriek tore the night, cut off by the dull sound of something falling to the worn carpet on the other side of Susan's door. That at least was not imagination.

The house awoke. Down the corridor or perhaps upstairs, one tentative door creaked opened, then another. A question voiced, then another. As she grabbed a shawl, other voices became the half-coherent babbling of men trying to whisper. A wash of light flooded under the door, then just as suddenly went out with a crash. Someone swore.

The voices were gathering, consulting, moving nearer. "What's going on? Where's Miss Pickering?" A knocking at her door. "Are you all right in there, Miss?"

"Oi! Something scratched me!" That high-pitched nervous chirp would be Miss Kennedy.

Bespectacled and slippered, the candle in her hand, Susan had just set her fingers to the latch when someone roared.

"Miss Pickering? Are you there!" That would be young Mr Nash.

"Of course I am here," Susan Pickering said, and dragged back on the handle.

It did not move. A quick glance assured her that no key stuck out usefully from the lock where she'd left it, nor had it fallen to the floor below.

Shaken she thought she heard a boot scrape the floorboards quite nearby, and a man's voice said, "Look again, sweeting."

"What?" she snapped, but as soon as she set down the lamp, there was the key. In the lock. Where it belonged. "Oh, for pity's sake!"

Either she was going mad or she needed new glasses, she thought, giving the key a hard twist— which shot the bolt home, locking the door. So it had been open all the time? Stuck then, swollen shut in the damp of a foggy summer night. When she rotated the key, the lock disengaged. She could see the thin line of light uninterrupted down the length of the door jamb, but still it held fast. No, not quite: it rattled slightly, as if someone leaning against it had stepped away chuckling.

Frustration mounting, Susan paced away, then returned, examining every seam of the door frame by the little light she had. She rattled and pounded, finally kicked at the door. Flakes of old paint dislodged, jumped, and floated like rose petals to her feet. No one came.

From the rising volume, every one of her lodgers, the maids, the cook and the boy Peter, everyone had gathered in front of her door exclaiming.

"Someone open this door!" she cried.

"Agh, blimey, that thing touched me!" Was that Mr Buttercomb?

"What thing?"

"What is going on?" Susan demanded, pounding until her fist hurt. Someone open this door, now!"

"It is gone. No, there it is! Do you see it?"

It was like the first scene of *Hamlet, Prince of Denmark*, all voices in the fog. Meanwhile within her spinster's bedchamber the air grew thick and chill, smelling of wintry earth and ashes.

"Why does no one answer!" The words popped from her as puffs of steam. "And why is it so cold?"

Ah, yes, the window was open, the white curtains moving sluggishly as mist spilled over the sill. Clutching her summer shawl more tightly to her shoulders, Susan marched round the narrow bed to slam down the sash. It too was stuck in place

"What the devil is going on?"

The strange voice chuckled again, louder this time.

"More than you know, fair maiden."

A breath on her cheek made her start, the sensation of cold fingers trapping her own, and a deep voice chuckling in her ear.

"Who is there?" she demanded, turning about. "Stand back. I have a pistol." Not on her person, but an intruder could not know that.

On the bed, the covers stirred, the mattress edge depressed and the same man's voice sang sweetly:

> *My maiden mistress come to me*
> *And many a gift I'll bear to thee.*

"Where are you," she commanded.

"Find me."

Snatching up the candle, she thrust it high, assaulting the shadows. No one, nothing but her own breath frosty in a room turned to ice.

"Show yourself!"

As she watched in wonder, tendrils of frost sprang up along her iron bedstead, springing across the bars and finials like swiftly growing vines. When she gasped, the air burned in her lungs like frostbite.

More fearful than she would admit, and more desperate, she turned and ran for the door, calling out to no avail.

"As ever, they hear thee not. You are nothing to them. Only their servant."

"I am the mistress of this house. Be gone. I do not fear you."

That was a lie.

"You have said otherwise in your dreams. Have I not lain there with thee?"

"Is this a dream?" she demanded as bravely as she could. "What are you?"

The icy hand grabbed her throat, stopped her voice. Froze the air in her lungs.

"Do you not know me?"

> *Wrens in the wood, fish in the flood.*
> *Sorrow walks with bone and blood,*
> *And you, dear maid, beside me.*

Susan tried to claw the away hand, invisible in the fragile light yet strangely substantial. If it were solid enough to hold her, she thought, then it must be solid enough to twist. The grip shifted just enough for her to croak:

"In God's name, leave me alone!"

Abruptly, she was released, the fingers springing away, and the entity—man, or ghost, whatever it was—hissed. But not the voice. Echoing now like an empty hall it rang again from every corner of the room.

> *Wrens in the wood, fish in the flood*
> *Sorrow shall walk with bone and blood*
> *And you, dear maid, abide me.*

"What's all this then?" A new voice boomed from somewhere below. The front door boomed closed. "What is going on up there? And where, if you please, is Miss Pickering?"

Oh, thank goodness, it was Donovan!

Hand at her aching chest, Susan sank to her knees. Donovan. Solid, sturdy Ned Donovan, sound as a summer day and home at last. His jovial presence advancing dispelled the hysteria with each firm step on the stair. Even the air in her chamber freshened as he came. By the time he gained the landing, the excitement had dropped to nothing more than a nervous cough and Miss Kennedy's sniffling.

From a throat much taxed with over-use, but with a touch of his customary good humor, the Irishman demanded, "Well?"

Near Susan's window an unmistakably foul oath exploded. She knew it was an oath even without recognizing the accent or many of the words. As much French as English, there was no mistaking the intent. Looking up, she thought she saw a glimmering light outlining a shadow near the ceiling. With it that dark mass, the ranting voice faded and dwindled like a candle guttering out under a bell jar.

"Yes, you should run, you villain," she rasped, and added a few terrible words no one imagined she knew.

"And let me ask again: where is Miss Pickering?" Donovan demanded, in the ringing tones that could cut across a Chartist rally.

"She— she don't answer, sir," Ellen stammered.

Standing in the dark, Miss Pickering said acidly: "If you please, Mr Donovan. I am—" A storm of voices exploded, and were just as suddenly silenced. "I am right here."

Under Donovan's hand, the latch clicked, and the door swung lightly in. Wide eyes turned her way limned in a dim chiaroscuro tableau. The young men, Mr Swindon and Mr Nash hovered with one flickering candle between them, and the irritable Mr Buttercombe hanging back. There was Mrs Nixon, the cook, her dour Scottish face set in frowns; young Peter, the dogsbody, trembling and doubly pale under his freckles. Even the aged Haliwells, whom one seldom saw, peered over the rail from the floor above like angels in their lofty aerie.

And at the center of them all, Miss Kennedy comforted the housemaid Ellen where they knelt over a crumpled heap on the carpet: Daisy, the younger maid, wrapped in the shreds of her nightgown.

At once relieved and furious, Miss Pickering's eyes automatically lifted to Donovan, a bowler hat tilted back, his collar askew beneath fiery whiskers. She tightened the cords of her dressing gown and started forward.

"What's happened to Daisy?"

"No, don't look."

"Mr Donovan—don't be ridiculous."

Her chilled hand caught his warm one briefly as she passed, but she had no time for a more cordial greeting. No time to be protected.

"Ellen, Peter," she snapped as she bent over the body. "Get some lights in here. The rest of you, stand away. Who has the candle? Mr Nash, over here, please."

Donovan reached across and took charge of the chimney lamp, casting the light where it would do the most good.

"Oh, such a look on her face!" Black curls bouncing out of her nightcap, Kitty Kennedy gasped through her tears. "As if she was frightened to death!"

Swift as a sparrow, Miss Pickering laid fingers on the maid's wrist and found it colder than her own, too cold and still. Leaning forward, she listened for breath, for the murmuring rhythm of the heart.

"Miss Kennedy, the *sal volatile* and a mirror, if you please."

"But she's dead!"

Nevertheless, the younger woman handed over a small vial and a pocket mirror, too from the pocket of her dressing gown.

"My dear girl," said Elias Nash, patting Kitty's shoulder while Swindon scowled. "It is all right. She's just had a fright, you'll see."

Miss Kennedy shook her head. The sharp bite of ammonia had caused no reaction, no sudden cough of breath and vitality. No mist formed on the mirror held to the little maid's mouth and nose. If any life remained in the girl, it was fast escaping and already beyond help. And as the gas lamps in the hall began to hiss and flare with light, it was plain that Kitty might not be wrong. For the look frozen on Daisy's face was one of open mouthed, wide-eyed terror, though not a mark appeared to be on her.

"She is dead, poor thing," said Miss Pickering, sitting back on her heels. "But . . . what on earth happened out here? Mr Nash, I heard your voice first of all. Were you impertinent with Daisy? If you frightened her in some way . . ."

"Miss Pickering, I protest!" An office clerk in his twenties, nerves already assaulted, Nash paled at the implication. "I was fast asleep, as well as anyone can sleep in this place. Besides, Swindon's been flirting with her."

"Here now! No one's mistreated her, certainly not I."

"Why did she scream then?"

"You said it was a ghost," the other young man sniffed. "Or someone did."

"A ghost!" Donovan murmured. "Now that is interesting."

"I never did. You told me to follow it."

"You said it touched you!"

"Stop it, both of you," Miss Pickering snapped, and they did.

"So it's ghosts, is it?" Mr Buttercombe, knitting anger out of a skein of nerves, edged away from the little crowd. "Serving girls frightened to death? Murdered, for all I know? Madness and mayhem. I did not come up to London to live in a haunted house, and I will not, Miss Pickering. Not for another day. I have had enough. I shall be leaving forthwith."

"Steady on, Buttercombe!" Swindon said with forced jollity. "Ghosts, forsooth! It might have been anything, a shadow from the street. An owl in the window."

"Or a body on the landing," Donovan reminded them. "The streets are filled with fog, sir, and there is no moon. You can't even see across the road. No shadows."

He rather hoped it was a ghost, because the alternative was that one of them had killed the girl. Murder might make a better story, especially if he worked in a spectral visitor, but Susan—Miss Pickering—wouldn't like the police tromping all over her house, causing talk among the neighbors.

"No." Mr Buttercombe was not open to argument. "I will not stay in this house another day. This derelict pile of yours is quite odd enough without gibbering spectres."

"I beg your pardon?"

"Aye, and so you should, Miss. So you—"

"Hark!" Swindon shouted. "What's that!"

The chime of the case clock below banged out. Unconsciously, every member of the household stopped to count off the twelve staves of midnight.

Grey as his nightshirt, Buttercombe yelped and pointed down into the foyer below.

"There it is! Can't you see it? Upon my soul, 'tis a hooded—a hooded monk, as clear as— Ah! It's gone! And so am I!"

"No gibbering, now, Buttercombe," said Donovan through a smirk.

"I shall write a letter to the Times!"

Beyond that, the man had nothing else to offer but a hasty retreat and the slam of his chamber door echoing in the passage. And now Ellen returned with a counterpane from the girl's bed to lay over her.

"Peter, what are you doing?" Donovan spoke into the shadows below the steep staircase. "Get back here!"

"I seen it, sir," Peter said from the bottom stair. "Looked me right in the eye and laughed like a loonie, it did, then went into the wall, there. "

"A ghost, you mean?" said Susan, getting to her feet.

The reporter looked where Peter pointed, as eager as anyone for an actual paraphysical experience, but if there was anything to see he had missed it.

Briskly Miss Pickering dispatched Peter to fetch the doctor, and prevailed upon Nash and Swindon to take Daisy decently up to her bed at the top of the house. Ellen, the tears tracking her cheeks, went ahead to show the way.

"Let's have a pot of tea for everyone, please, Mrs Nixon," said the mistress of the house. And that was everyone sorted.

Donovan admired her brisk, unsentimental management of the household. Her steadiness seemed almost a force of nature. Of magic, even. He also quite liked the sway of the linen nightgown above her bare ankles as she led the way downstairs.

Gathered round the table in the parlour that was their common room, they all sat over sweet milky tea exclaiming with horrible enthusiasm while nerves steadied. Donovan asked easy, casual questions, getting them to share, as friends do, while he listened. There might be little enough, but it was his nature and his calling to collect details. The little family never noticed how neatly they were being interviewed.

Then the constable arrived, and Dr Moreton, at last, somewhat cross at being called out in the dead of night over a servant. Meeting them at the door, Mr Donovan did all the talking, shielding Miss Pickering as the world expected a man to do in matters of mortality. Much to Donovan's surprise, she allowed him to do it without her usual prickles—almost without noticing— and excused herself. He watched her go, half inclined to call her back, to keep her by him. Her expression had altered over the past hour, her composure showing the strain.

The doctor examined the body, more or less, asked a few perfunctory questions; the young constable, with rather less *sang froid,* asked a few more, to all of which Donovan gave calm, vague answers. No mention was made of ghosts, although the Irishman sensed they were being watched by something unwholesome all the while.

In short order the doctor wrote out a death certificate declaring the maid's demise to be of natural causes, a sudden brain fever, and that was a relief, of sorts. Ned even paid the doctor himself, and tipped the constable for his good will, and saw them both out.

When he had locked the door behind them, he followed the murmur of voices back to the parlor with an old song going round in his head. Passing the tall pedal harp as he entered, the strings stirred, and words took shape in his mind.

> *Now is the month of Maying*
> *When merry lads are playing!*
> *Fa-la-la la-la la-la*

He hated that song, but there it was going round and round. A girl was dead, the lively tune with its lisping fa-la-las struck him as violently offensive.

Then the white haired Haliwells, hand in hand, greeted him on their way to bed, and it was gone.

"Good night, Mr Donovan," they chorused. And old Mr Haliwell added, "I hope you find it."

"Hm, yes, good night," Ned murmured automatically

Among the rest, the bickering and brittle laughter, the shying at shadows, had already become yawns and good-nights. The other young men shuffled out, followed by Kitty and Ellen who leaned on one another, sniffling across the class divide. Clicks and bangs echoed above, the Irishman slid the parlour door closed with a thump, and the house resumed an uneasy peace.

Scandalous it surely was, the two of them alone in the middle of the night behind a closed door, with staid Miss Pickering all naked in her nightdress. But he was a gentleman, of a kind, and besides, weren't they were as good as betrothed already? Powerful magic had bonded them in this room once; surely that bond still held.

"Miss Pickering? Susan!" Donovan said. Alone together as they so rarely were, the formality slipped easily away. "What's the matter?"

Elbows propped on the table, a painted teacup halfway to her lips, she had fallen into a kind of reverie, silent and removed. Though her eyes were closed, a line of tension clenched her jaw, and the tea cup was gripped between white knuckled hands. That she breathed was evident, though her chest rose and fell only shallowly under her nightdress.

"Susan," he said, very gently.

"Ah, don't!" she gasped, before realizing whose hands were prizing her fingers away from the cup.

"You won't want to break that, eh?"

"Oh, yes, I mean no. That is— Were you talking before? Or singing... no you can't have been. I thought—" Blinking rapidly Susan cleared her throat and shook herself out of the trance, or whatever it had been. "I fancied you were telling me a story. It was horrible, but I couldn't make you stop!"

"It can't have been me then, can it?" he teased, and drew her over to the worn sofa in the palm-crowded alcove. Putting a glass of sherry in her hand he said, "A dream is all it is. You'll have dozed off."

"Where were you?"

He told her briefly, and added, "The question is, where were you?"

III
Analysis

SUSAN LET HER GAZE FOLLOW his movement about the room as he opened drawers, lifted cushions, moved photographs here and there, though for what reason she couldn't fathom. After a minute, he removed his jacket, one of the three muted plaids in today's striking ensemble. He rolled back his cuffs to keep them clean as he set to refreshing the fire.

She could admit, were she honest, that he was a fine looking man: a tall, sturdily built fellow, as loose limbed and well balanced as one of those prizefighters one saw in Hyde Park. How odd it was that even as she sat trembling in the house of her childhood, he seemed as comfortable in it as if they had lived here together for years. There was something steadying in his routine, the economical movements, the melancholy tune sung just under his breath. She might almost forget—

She forced her eyes elsewhere, feeling ridiculous. What had happened to her composure? Where had Sensible Susan got to, and who was this wretched lovesick girl mooning in her place? She had come to terms with her spinsterhood long ago. Fond of Ned Donovan she might be, but his periodic invitations to elope to Gretna Green were ludicrous, even unkind to a plain, dowerless girl past her prime. Certainly not to be taken seriously.

She sipped the sherry, hardly tasting it, the chill untouched. Donovan's fire had caught well, flames danced above the coals, but Susan felt enveloped by cold. Long, deep breaths wreathed her in mist, and when she looked saw the flames had stopped moving, their dance suspended.

"Have you heard this?" the mocking voice in sang her ear. "I have a mighty cock that croweth up the day. He maketh me risen early my Matins for to say."

A hazy image had shaped out of the haze, transparent as a memory. A man stood before her, arms open in welcome. A tonsure of shaggy curls ringed the head, and when he saw her shift her glance aside, Susan thought the merry eyes widened in surprise.

"What are you?"

The sensual mouth curled, then he thrust himself closer.

"My cock's eye is bright as crystal, for all he never slumbers. And every night he perches within my lady's chamber. If you take my meaning, little maiden. And do you, then, my little hen?"

Hardly more than a whisper, only one word escaped. "Edward!"

Undismayed, the creature went on in a voice like the wind on ice. "I have a little hen, her eyes are filled with fire. What rhymes with fire, my chickens?"

Not a single entity answered but four or five women speaking at once, high and sweet, old and young. Lithe figures swirled through the mist.

"Choir! Desire! Funeral pyre!"

"And will you have a new hen to be your sister?"

"Yes, master, yes!"

Six ghostly women's voices wreathed around each other, sighing as they chanted. She could feel the breeze of their ethereal bodies dancing around her, binding her.

"What of her lover?" the master catechized.

"Be still!" commanded Susan between clenched teeth. They would harm Edward if they could. She would not let that happen. "Leave him alone."

> *We hear her, night by holy night,*
> *a-sighing of his name.*
> *She lewdly counts o'er all his parts,*
> *his hands and mouth the same,*
> *and waist and thigh. Oh my! Oh my!*
> *Fa la la-la lah! ah! ah!*

They fell to sighing, swooning, giggling while the man's voice babbled more lewd nonsense.

"Whilst he lies in the room above, shamed as a maiden, pale as a worm, afraid to thrust him twixt her canting thighs, the cock upon the hen, that's he with lewd and weeping eye. Oh, he would creep between her naked sheets to teach her harlotry."

Mustering whatever energies might be left to her, Susan balled her fists and stood up. She would not be terrorized!

"Stop it!" she rasped feeling the blood rush into her face, her hands shaking. The mocking voices melted away like ice in summer. The fire crackled and popped.

It was not real. It could not be real. Only fancies born of magic and exhaustion. And of watching Donovan. Imagining Donovan.

"What's that?" Donovan asked brightly, wiping his sooty hands on the last of her mother's fine linen table napkins,

"Nothing," she snapped.

Concerned, he returned to take her hand and pull her down beside him on the sofa, offering the sherry glass like a tonic.

"You're awfully cold for 'nothing', *mo chroí*."

What was there to say? Fear had swept over her twice tonight, and it was comforting to have his strength so nearby. His warmth and the sherry's would be enough, she thought. No need to involve him in her distasteful hallucinations.

"I've spoken with all the others," he reminded her gently. "Now it is your turn, eh? Tell me what happened to you when Daisy died. Only you were alone."

"I can't, I—" Sensible Susan straightened her back and adjusted her spectacles, breathing slowly to restore her composure. "It's complicated."

"You're clever. Explain it to me."

Feeling his eyes on each movement of her unremarkable hands, she threw her long braid back over her shoulder, cleared her throat. She was not crying—Susan Pickering did not waste her tears on nerves and shapeless doubts—but he had the effrontery to tuck his clean handkerchief into the sleeve of her dressing gown, all the same.

Pretending his fingers had not grazed her wrist, she met his grey-eyed regard and took a breath, and told him everything, or nearly so.

"You remember the sketchbook, the one Mr Fitzroy," she began, her voice almost a whisper, "the one he enchanted?"

Donovan nodded, slightly surprised. At Christmas just passed, they had both been of some service to a young fellow of that name who claimed—and proved—to be a lord of Faerie. His idle touch had altered the perfectly common book so that, sometimes, the things Susan drew on its pages took on a kind of shadow life and moved like the images in a zoetrope machine.

He had seen it himself, clear enough to send him running to the Crystal Palace on a frozen Christmas Eve to offer help. He didn't think she had opened it since that night.

"I was drawing and . . ."

"You saw Daisy's death?"

"No!" she said, pulling her shawl around her again. "Oh God, how horrible! Though, perhaps if I had . . . If it had shown me, I might have . . ."

Reluctantly she laid out the last bit of her terror: trapped, isolated, taunted by the night breeze, menaced by a ghastly whisper, and the fingers of ice clutching her throat.

To her surprise, he listened with the same sober attention he had given all the others, watching intently as she described the locked door, the insinuating voice, the chanted threats. When Donovan spoke, it was to urge her to continue, not to tell her what it meant.

"It was horrible," she concluded.

A shudder of panic rippled across her skin, too icy for a summer night. Without asking, he slipped her arm through his, entwined his warm fingers with her cold ones.

"A man in your room, was it?" he asked, keeping his tone light. "Should I be jealous?"

"Be sensible, Ned Donovan. As soon as I heard your voice, he was gone. Or nearly."

"I shall always be your champion."

She thought, "And I yours," but harbouring her uncertainties she said, "My flower of chivalry. But you cannot be with me every moment."

"Of course I can, when we're married and not causing a scandal in the middle of the night."

Staring across to the gleaming fireplace, Susan let loose a sigh. "So I am to put down my keys and dash about the world with you, knitting your socks in railway carriages and washing them in dreary hotels?"

"Yes." His eyes sparkled.

"Nursing your fevers in Persia or Peru?"

"And Timbuktu and far Samarkand, yes!"

"A life of pure romance."

"We'll have the faery sketchbook with us. Who knows what we might find?" Laughing, he lightly kissed her cheek, and she did not flinch.

"This is how we know I am the sensible one, and you are the lunatic." Thinking, waiting, she finally said, "But what did Daisy see?"

"And that's the real question tonight, isn't it. Tell me, *a cushla*, has this house always been haunted?"

"Haunted!" Susan scoffed. "But none of that was real. Only midnight fancies and a warped old door." But she knew it was not that. A shiver sent her to stand at the glowing hearth, warming her hands.

"Every old house makes noises in the night. Mice in the walls become monsters under the bed."

"And don't I know that too well, that grew up in the bishop's house at Rathnaclare. Black shadows lurk in sunny rooms, and doors slam with no one opening them."

Susan nodded with the beginnings of a smile. Talk of magic often underscored the Irish patterns in his speech.

"Yes. And rising damp under the wallpaper breathes out a white lady, especially to a child waking in the night. How easy is a bush supposed a bear? But no ghosts that I know of, until tonight, if that's what it is."

"Peter saw something."

"A child waking in the night," Susan repeated.

"Nash and Swindon?"

"Oh, they egg each other on. They might say anything to impress Miss Kennedy. If it had been no one else, we could dismiss their ghost as a mouse in the wall."

"A mouse in the wall did not kill the maid."

"No," Susan said, taking some thought. "She seemed a sensible girl. Not as steady as Ellen, but still, I wouldn't have said she was given to fancies."

"Do I sense some doubt?"

"She had been nervous, lately, now that I think of it. Forgetful and clumsy. Sleeping badly, according to Ellen, and given to nightmares. I came upon her in this room yesterday. Her hand was raised to dust the harp, but Daisy simply stood there with the strangest look. I had to say her name twice, and . . . Oh!"

Susan shook her head picturing the bloodless face, a painted mask in her mind's eye. "And in the end, that horrible scream. As if something had torn out her heart."

"Could it have been an ordinary man? Did she have any followers?"

"Only I!" murmured the hollow voice only she could hear.

"One or two," Susan said, defying the dancing whisper, "but what man could have frightened her so much, or vanished so completely?"

"Or walked through a wall?"

IV
Escalation

AFTER A SUBDUED BREAKFAST, the young people went off to their daily toil. True to his word, Mr Buttercombe settled up and swept out with his collar half-buttoned and not even a cup of tea. Ellen reported that Mr Donovan had left for the City at daybreak with a promise to return the same day.

Miss Pickering had accounts to do, a task the more strained by having to pay the undertaker who came to take poor Daisy away. When that was done, she wrote out her requirement for a general housemaid, and sent Ellen round to the domestics registry to see about a replacement, which left her lacking not one but two maids for half a day. It felt heartless but the house could not stop running while she mourned.

Then she spent a sorrowful half-hour composing a letter to Daisy's father in deepest Sussex. It would be days before she had any reply from him, if ever, and even then she would have to absorb the funeral costs.

A funeral. She'd never had to respond to a servant's death before, not as mistress of her own house. The details after her great uncle Erasmus' violent[2] death had been managed by his sister's butler. What was customary? Should she cover the mirrors or simply turn them to the wall? Almost before she could finish the thought, here was Peter staggering down from the attic under a box of black gauze, and muttering that they had enough ghosts already without Daisy's spirit, bless her, keeping everyone awake.

It would have to do. Susan changed into an old gown and pinner, and helped the boy before attacking at least part of the Thursday cleaning that would otherwise be left undone. At least it

---

[2] Related in *King's Raven*

was not laundry day. With luck, Ellen would be home soon with a steady, sober, hardworking girl who could manage a needle and didn't mind the odd apparition.

It was half past five before Donovan returned home again. With a cheerful urgency, he dropped his hat and went calling Susan's name through the house. He found her at last in Mrs Knox's spotless kitchen, linen sleeves rolled up to her elbows, collapsed around a mug of tea. Her hair in long strands had escaped her cap, and ashes smudged her face and throat.

"Is it you, Cinderella?" he asked, sliding into a chair across from her.

"Only if you have brought my golden slippers," said Susan without moving. "Or I cannot go to the ball."

Nearby, Mrs Nixon snapped at Peter to stop making a mess with the coal scuttle.

Donovan waited until Susan glanced up at him through red-rimmed eyes, blinked, pushed a lock of fallen hair behind her ear with no hope of its staying put.

"You are not to look at me, sir," she said faintly, hiding her hands under the polishing cloth. "Go away."

"Where else should I look?" he said, meaning it. Twitching the cloth aside, he lifted her reddened hands to his lips. "You are the fairest in the land, *mo chroí*, and you'll never persuade me otherwise."

Then he was holding her hands and whispering the words every woman longs to hear, but not when she's exhausted and every muscle aches: "I should like very much to take you to tea."

"Ned, dearest, not now."

Almost before she knew what she had said, the startling endearment was hanging in the air between them in front of witnesses and the man himself, grinning under his fiery mustache. Susan let out a groan of mortification and hid her face in her hands, but they both knew she had crossed her Rubicon. Her temples were pounding and her chin was smudged, and she only hoped he would not propose again. Not now, when she was clearly not in her right mind.

By the look of him, he already had and she had just said yes, or would soon enough, and he was probably right. Smug, conceited Irishman!

Mrs Nixon, too, had gone silent. When the seconds passed without further eaves to drop, she muttered some incomprehensible malediction, and bustled her sharp Scottish nose out the kitchen door, and they were alone.

"You'll be wanting a bonnet, love," said Donovan.

Abruptly Susan, charged by her own chagrin, pushed back her chair. Deftly she slipped past him clutching the rags of her maidenly decorum about her.

"When I've arrayed myself respectably, Mr Donovan, I do have one or two errands in the village. You may accompany me, if you like."

He had just closed the door and come in with the afternoon post in his hands when she swept up in a dark green gown over a narrow crinoline, and a freshly scrubbed face under her second-best bonnet.

"What have you got there? Mr Donovan, are you snooping?"

"Professional prerogative, Miss. Here's the Weekly Misery for Mrs Nixon, what rubbish. Something virile for Nash—*hmm,* let's see." Humming lightly, he peered under the plain brown wrapper. "Ah! *'The Manly Art of Self Defense,'* is it? Good lad. Very improving. And here's a pale pink envelope addressed in a feminine hand for Swindon, and yes, delicately scented with rosewater. Probably not his aged mum, eh? And this for you."

He teased her with a fat packet from a pair of solicitors, her name flowering across the face of it. "I assume that is your own dear self, that being the style of your full Christian name. We'll need that for crying the banns."

"*Tsk*, crying the banns, indeed." She snatched the packet away from him and let it drop onto the chipped Chinese dish that normally received the mail. "Why do you keep asking when you already know the answer?"

"It is my burden in life to know when people mean what they say, and I can tell that you, my dear girl, do not. Even Peter agrees with me. Or if you do mean it, the conclusion doesn't make you happy And so I live in hope."

"You live in a fantasy." Then, because she feared, or felt, or knew he was right, she focused on thrusting a hand into a glove, smoothing it as she went. "Ned, really, it's no use. You must not think . . ."

"Susan, *a cushla,*" Gallantly he raised her one ungloved hand to his lips, his eyes all the while on hers. "If you will keep giving me my name in front of people, what else can I do?"

If her heart fluttered like some silly girl in one of Mrs Nixon's penny dreadfuls, it would be because she'd got too little sleep and too much excitement the night before. Yes, that was it.

"Let's be off then," said Susan, chasing the fluster from her voice as he took her arm and stepped away.

As he always did on leaving the house, Donovan touched his hat lightly to the faerie wood across the road, hoping the little folk who lived there would take note and be pleased.

He considered, too, the very last thing Mr Fitzroy's American friend had told him before the odd pair had vanished, words like a command out of the Fair Country itself: "You marry that girl!" Mr Harper had said, and Donovan meant to. He hardly dared to do otherwise.

Donovan set a brisk pace until Susan, breathless, stopped dead still in the road and let him carry on alone. Fortunately for them both, he missed the pleasant weight of her hand on his arm within a few seconds. Stopped, apologized and returned. At a more leisurely stroll they began again, remarking blandly on the weather.

"And here we are, walking out together like any courting couple," he beamed.

The village wasn't far, just a mile or so down the gentle slope through tall old trees past large, respectable houses. They skirted the tailored lawns of Alleyn's College and chose a shorter path that rose through the remnant of the ancient wood that had once crowned all of Sydenham Hill. Shorter it was but still long enough, all in all, for the reporter to describe what he'd learned that morning, which he told with his usual flair.

He had risen early, so he said, to have his coffee among the jumbled files at the newspaper's basement, a grim collection of cabinets and boxes they called the morgue. Finding more clues than certainties had led him to wait impatiently at the British Museum for a man called Kemble to arrive. The result had been remarkably satisfying, for Kemble had not only found the maps and records he needed, but troubled to help him puzzle out what they meant. Still, it was not enough to explain what had happened. For that, Kemble had recommended a chat with the vicar of St Bartholomew's in Dulwich, where they happened to be going at this exact moment.

"Well now," he said at last. You recall me asking how long had your house been haunted, and you pretending it never was."

"I, what? I did what?"

"Well, I'll tell you, shall I?" he went on gleefully. "For one thing, it wasn't always called Hollytree House. In fact, it wasn't always a house."

That she found easy to accept. London town and the country round about it existed in a perpetual state of change. The city had long ago outgrown its walls and was now swarming up through Penge and Lambeth, villages linked to the metropolis by new railway lines tearing across the southern hills that rose gently away from the Thames. Dulwich itself would be next, no doubt. Streets round about were being conscientiously paved and lighted. The first gas street lamps had been installed a year or two before when the Crystal Palace rose in the district.

"Now tell me, love, how old is Hollytree House?"

"Not so very old. Eighty or a hundred years, I think. Why?"

His grin, infectious as it was, brightened her spirits as much as the fresh air.

"Ah, older than that, you'll find, though it's been made over twice or three times. It has old roots, said yer man Kemble. The foundations of the current house were laid in 1563, according to the plot we found once we got to the Records Office. But if we were to look about for boundary markers, we'd likely find ourselves in a medieval convent or priory, hundreds of years older. There's your hooded character, eh? And who's to say what went on there beneath your back parlour."

"I shudder to think!"

He could feel her suit the action to the word.

"Now your father, Gideon Pickering, solicitor, must have bought the house shortly before his marriage. The record is unclear and some pages are missing."

Susan's face paled within the safety of her bonnet. Of course there were pages missing. If only he would stop digging about in things that didn't matter. Thankfully, her personal history was not Donovan's goal at the moment, but once started, she knew the reporter would worry the thing like a dog with an old shoe.

"In such an old place, and with your gifts, you must have heard or seen things as a child, apparitions or footsteps in the night?"

"No."

"Voices, then, or furniture flung about. Bed curtains torn open at midnight, maybe? A bride locked in a window seat on her wedding night, never seen again?"

"Good heavens, no! How dreadful!"

Walking a bit further in companionable silence, they greeted a couple of their neighbors coming the other way. Further on, they stepped aside for a child and her governess taking the air on a pair of plump ponies. Mr Donovan tipped his hat and Miss Pickering smiled pleasantly, trying to recall their names.

Alone again, she said thoughtfully, "There was a white lady, for awhile, who paced the halls. But she went away when I was a child. Or perhaps when I lost my fear of the dark and grew out of her. There might have been others, I suppose. After my mother died, and all the servants left . . ."

But no. That tale was for another time, or not at all. If Donovan noticed her hesitation, he made no remark.

The path curved eventually into what must be the middle of the wood where several paths crossed among the close-grown trees. Only dappled light filtered through the tall elms and poplars, but beneath them a treasure bloomed.

"Oh, Edward, look!" Susan exclaimed, her face alight. "Bluebells!"

One gloved hand on his arm for balance, Susan stooped to bring up a few of the blossoms nodding on their stalks. From one of them a tiny, almost human face peered out, glaring and chittering like a disgruntled chipmunk.

"My goodness, I do beg your pardon!" she said, curtsying politely. "I did not know. Yes, I shall be more mindful from now on."

When she opened her hand, it flitted away with dragonfly speed.

"Stand very still, if you please," Donovan said, his whole body on guard. "I believe . . . Yes."

From nowhere they could see, it popped into the air above her cheek and bestowed a tiny kiss just in the corner of her mouth, another in the corner of her eye, which left a faint white star behind and made her sigh. Subtly, the light under the trees brightened, the murk cleared away, and with no more than a thought, they had entered the Borderland.

Hovering at the level of the Irishman's grey gaze, the faery creature seemed to take his measure, or the measure of his ruddy hair and whiskers. It whistled and piped with apparent admiration and then in mid-air, performed a twirling figure the reporter thought must be a kind of curtsey. Then lightly it touched the smooth space between his brows.

A single "Oh!" marked the change in his awareness as well. Gallantly, he removed his hat and bowed in his own less frolicsome way.

Apparently pleased, the bluebell faery darted off whistling in trills and shrills, leaving both mortals in a state of awe-filled grace.

"Perhaps we should be going on," Susan whispered.

Hand in hand, they climbed the meandering path, neither remarking how wonderful it was that both had understand the faery, though its speech was nothing like English, and its gestures curious.

"What was that all about I wonder," Donovan said quietly, still struck by the experience.

"A blessing, I think," said Susan. "Or else a warning."

"Or both?"

The path ended in a flat stone footbridge where a trickle of the little river Effra briefly surfaced from its dark confines under the hill. At the bridge end cluttered with broken, discarded brick and crumbled mortar from an nearby construction sites, Donovan shaped Susan's waist between his big hands and swung her gently to the ground. They emerged from the leafy walks into the noise and rush of a busy high street that rumbled up to greet them.

It was an old place, this village, long occupied, and the well stocked shops, the bank, both pubs, and all the rest had strong roots, growing out and around Alleyn's School. With the great city swarming up from the towards them, though, it might well be overtaken by great London itself soon. Around a bend in the road, new terraced houses and a fine hotel were shaking off the newness of their first coats of paint. With the railway and the Crystal Palace so near by, it was becoming a proper town already.

A quick call at the post office to pay the gas subscription was accomplished with efficient dispatch. Similarly, visits to the butcher and the ironmongers, which had recently become a general mercantile. They greeted the neighbors they knew and smiled politely at the few who stared. Miss Pickering had never been seen walking out with a man not a relation, and never with a smile on her face, that anyone could recall.

Good humour and gentle magic had made them both drop their guard. Good company left them unprepared for what came next.

At Bremerton's, the stationers, Susan dawdled as she always did over fine letter paper before choosing the cheapest that could still be called respectable and a bottle of decent ink. Ned Donovan, eager to call on the vicar, expressed a certain impatience, but no teasing or cajolery on his part could urge her to any haste.

Who knew there could be so many sizes, shapes, and qualities of paper to choose from. And pencils of varying weights and thickness, graphite, charcoal, and wax and oh my goodness, colors! With little to spend and quite certain such things were more than she deserved, Susan sighed and selected two quite ordinary pencils.

Once among the sketchbooks, Ned acknowledged defeat, retiring to a step-ladder beside the door where he could watch her. Susan hardly noticed.

Some of the books were merely bound paper with parchment covers, others stitched with good linen paper especially for water colors and covered in kid as fine as her mother's best gloves, and just as expensive. But then, oh then! She found it.

The black calf-bound book with rounded corners was the perfect size to fit in her handbag. The narrow strap and pewter button would keep it from flying open, and a cunning little pocket in the back cover would doubtless be useful. The unlined paper felt as if it would welcome both pencil and ink. Being French, it was a bit more dear than the plain ones, but surely its many useful features justified the extra sixpence.

When, arms filled, she finally arrived at the counter, Susan found a small pile of other, finer items already being bundled in brown paper and tied up with string. She glanced longingly at the rainbow array of colored pencils as they disappeared into their wrapping.

"I saw you looking at them."

She looked up to find Donovan leaning on one elbow, beaming at her. How she could have missed him, dressed in that much plaid, she did not know.

"And the letter paper, too? And *that* ink! Mr Donovan, really, the cost! I cannot permit it."

"Ah, but neither can you prevent me, Miss Pickering, since we are practically engaged. I say, Bremerton, put all the lady's things, on my account, if you please." He winked, and whispered conspiratorially. "I wrangled a bonus out of MacKay this morning in Fleet Street. 'Jewel Theft and Foul Murder in Mayfair', remember?"

"Yes, but—"

No, she would be gracious, and grateful too. Unused to gifts, all she could do was smile under downcast eyes, and blush when he took her hand. Then squeak when all the colored pencils suddenly exploded from their wrapping as Mr Bremerton's assistant fumbled with the string. Donovan tried to sweep them into his arms, but every one escaped, bouncing, rolling, clattering over the floor.

Steel pens in neat boxes likewise leapt to freedom; letter openers, calendars, diaries flew open, pages fluttering as if a great wind had set them off; and some indeed flew birdlike out the door when it banged open, the bell jangling wildly overhead.

"What is it!" cried Mr Bremerton. "What's going on?" The young assistant burst into tears and dived under the counter. "You come back here and close that door, boy. And tidy all this up!"

An ink bottle rattled; its fellows on the same shelf trembled in sympathy.

Susan shrieked, "Stop it!"

"It isn't me," Donovan shouted.

"No, look!"

Spindly goblin limbs and splayed goblin fingers were wrapped around an India ink bottle and working at the tightly stoppered cap under two squidgy faces grinning like gargoyles. Others leapt and soared or bounced like balloons about the room setting up a rattling cacophony.

Glass was beginning to crack.

Donovan gripped Susan's hand and mildly addressed the proprietor, "We'll just be on our way. Send our purchases round to Hollytree House, if you please."

"But what about all this damage, Mr Donovan?" the man shouted back.

"Damage?" said Ned Donovan, slightly startled. "What damage? Good day!"

Taking her cue and his arm, Miss Pickering waited while Mr Donovan opened the door, though it nearly flew out of his hand. Together they walked out as placidly as if nothing at all had happened.

The door slammed, the bell jangled, the whirl of goods collapsed, and all was silence. Risking a look, Donovan saw the stationer, red-faced and gasping, flick the lock behind them and draw down the blind, just before collapsing to the wooden stool in terrorized exhaustion. The boy had already decamped.

"Does this happen often to you, Miss Pickering?" Donovan asked. "Ghosts, faeries, now poltergeists, or whatever they are?"

"Never," she whispered, catching her breath as they crossed the road.

"Never at all?" he frowned in return. "what has changed then, I wonder."

"My life was a genteel spinster's tedious round of watercolors and Charitable Works, until you came along, Mr Donovan."

"Until the day I found you freezing in the snow, you mean, all covered in faery kisses."

So frightening then, the image and everything that had come afterward made her laugh now. "Exactly. The change is you, I fear."

"The two of us together are a rare match. And look, here's Mariani's. Cream teas a specialty." Truth to tell, he would rather have stopped in at The Greyhound next door where the drinks were somewhat stronger but the company less refined.

"Edward, hush!" Susan put up a gloved hand . "Listen!"

A high brittle sound like children's laughter bubbled up from somewhere in the grassy verge, a sound Susan had not heard in months. Usually the laughter rang out merrily, filled with mischief. Today, she thought, a darker note prevailed.

"Do you hear it?" she asked.

Her friend nodded, his eyes scanning the road, the gathering sky, the shadows deepening under the eaves. Broad daylight and hard packed earth should have protected them, but the summer sky was shot with clouds harried by a still breeze aloft.

With every step Susan felt besieged by shadows like thrown spears from the cloud banks, too many for the slanting sunbeams to drive off. Dazzled, the lights sparkled in her eyes and no, she was determined not to faint. "There is something in the air, hiding," she said. "I wonder what will happen if I . . ."

Standing quite still, she raised a gloved hand to touch the fairy star near her eye, and stared directly into the shadows pooling around her skirts. Her mouth tightened. There they were, writhing creatures like wisps of gilded smoke drinking up the light.

She placed her hand on Donovan's and, from his sharp intake of breath, knew he could see them as well.

"Well, I'll be— What are they, do you think?"

"His minions, no doubt—that ghost or demon. They are trying to harry me into going home."

"That ghost of yours has a long reach."

"Does he? I will not be ordered about by him! Leave us, I command you," she said, then clapped her hands, just once, and they scattered away

She looked up at her friend. "I should very much like that cup of tea, now."

"As would I," Donovan agreed, though he would have much preferred to stop in at The Greyhound after all. "And possibly a quick exorcism, as well."

Searching her face, he nearly burst out laughing, for he realized she was more angry than frightened. If anything, the tight line of her lips showed her only more determined.

"The vicar's housekeeper makes a fine cup of tea," she said.

"The parsonage, Miss Pickering?"

"And quickly, Mr Donovan."

"And eventually you will tell me what just happened."

"I do hope so."

Sensing a deeper promise, Donovan whistled up the single hackney cab dozing near the pub, and they trotted up the high street.

V
Intelligence

THEY WERE STILL SLIGHTLY HILARIOUS when the maid let them in at the pristine white door of the vicar's modest home across from St Barnabas' church. There was no telling what other adventure they might have encountered had they continued walking that short distance, but all in all they were grateful to have missed it.

With barely enough time to compose themselves they were swiftly ushered into the book-lined presence of the Reverend Dr Marmion Frane. Apart from the dog collar, he might have been any elderly bachelor of scholarly inclination. A pink, balding head was framed in white close-cropped hair and fronted, under the customary steel spectacles, with the perpetual frown of a man who has spent his life more with books than with people. He looked up from his desk in surprise as Miss Pickering, whom he saw regularly, entered his study in the company of a robust and extravagantly bewhiskered young fellow he did not know. The prim lips drew back in a tight smile as he rose.

Introductions all around, tea called for, and biscuits. Miss Pickering and her companion discreetly settled at opposite ends of a rather fine settee. She breathed deeply of the calming scent of cut flowers and old books, and surprised the vicar by requesting a modest burial for one of her maids who had passed away quite suddenly in the night. That would, he surmised, explain the sense of portent that had entered with her.

The usual questions, then. No, Miss Pickering was not aware of any burial club funds or other pre-arrangements. This was confirmed by a nod from the somewhat distracted Mr Donovan with whom Dr Frane had expected to speak about something else entirely.

Yes, a brief graveside service in a corner of the churchyard would be both sufficient and economical. Even for a well loved servant, Miss Pickering was in no position to be extravagant, as Dr Frane was well aware.

Miss Pickering did not immediately offer any information surrounding the maid's death, and the vicar did not enquire. He had already heard rumours, some quite incredible. The arch look over his glasses, fraught with meaning, she returned coolly. Nevertheless, Dr Frane scratched a note in his diary and confirmed the standard fee of six pounds eight shillings and ninepence for the undertaker's plainest hearse plus two gravediggers, the hire of some wax flowers, and fees to the church itself, noting that the spinster paled but did not demur. That was something.

"Now then," said the vicar, laying down his pen. "That's settled. But a funeral, however essential, is not the sole reason for your coming here, is it Miss Pickering?"

His meaningful look transferred to Mr Donovan, who had been taking a turn around the room examining bookshelves with a writer's eye. Then the tea arrived with three kinds of scones, both jam and cream, which led to a fussing with cups and pots and sugar tongs that provided cover for telling glances, whispered questions, surreptitious touches.

Better late than never, so it is, thought Dr Frane, recalling his own long ago courtship. They would come to him for wedding instruction soon enough. If they were not yet ready, he thought he could guess what else concerned the girl.

When she had settled again, Donovan carried his cup away to study a display case filled with family pictures and souvenirs. She could see him in the corner of her eye, head cocked, humming an old hymn under his breath. After a moment he was content to stand by an open window, sipping tea in the most genteel manner possible.

"You want to know about your house, I expect," said Dr Frane.

A light click was Donovan's cup sharply meeting the saucer. "What makes you say that, sir?" the reporter asked quietly.

"I have been waiting for Miss Pickering to ask about it ever since she came into her inheritance."

"Another time, Dr Frane!" Susan snapped, adding a hasty apology. That, too, would wait.

"As you like, as you like. Perhaps it is too personal, as yet. I admit I had hopes when you introduced Mr Donovan— No? I suspect it will not wait much longer, whether it pleases you or not, Miss Pickering."

The vicar launched a sharp glance at each of his visitors before continuing smoothly. "You'll be back soon enough, or I miss my guess. But for now, yes, you wish to know about the house, and as it happens, I have kept notes over the years, preparing for my book on the legends and lore of the borough."

He had a steel pen in one hand with which he inscribed the date on a pristine new page in his notebook, and waited, poised to begin.

"Let us waste no more time. Please tell me what you already know or believe, and why you are looking into the history."

When she did not speak, he gazed over the half-moon spectacles to find her apparently sharing some silent communication with her friend.

"My dear? Or no, I see. Mr Donovan. I expect your keen reporter's mind will already have prepared the preliminary research in an orderly fashion, yes. Do go on."

There was no help for it. There was no way to ask without telling the whole story: Daisy's death, the apparitions, the terror in the house. Frane nodded, as if he had expected some such thing

By the time Donovan had finished, Dr Frane had filled up three pages in his neat public school hand, and a kind of scholarly ecstasy had brought a rosy glow to his pink scalp.

"Excellent, excellent, you are an efficient narrator, Mr Donovan. Almost as neat and surely as entertaining as the chroniclers of old. In fact, you may be interested to know that in the reign of King Alfred the Great . . . Let me see."

With this remark he went to a tall cupboard and drew out a very old folio bound in carved leather over boards. It had once been secured with buckled straps, but now he untied the string that held it together like a mailing parcel, and cleared a space for it on his desk. While scanning the parchment pages for quite a few anxious minutes, he made a long procedure, almost without looking, of pouring milk and tea, stirring in exactly two spoons of sugar, which he then slurped as he turned another page.

Susan nudged his attention, praying for patience. "Dr Frane?"

As neatly as if he were dictating a sermon, the Reverend Dr Frane laid out the additional facts, rumours, and lore he had gleaned from years of study and a great deal of speculation.

Illuminating Donovan's remarks, he revealed that Hollytree House was only the latest in a series of buildings on foundations that went back to the Dark Ages. The oldest structure had been a convent of cloistered nuns dedicated to St Audrey in the eleventh century. Perched on the banks of a now vanished river, it had been neither a rich nor a famous house, but a sturdy cloister for twelve holy maidens. Deposited by their families in fulfillment of a vow, or to spare the trouble of a dowry, or sometimes the fruit of an unfortunate liaison, they sang and prayed, stitched altar cloths and baked communion bread for the monks across the valley at the abbey of St Cuthbert. For centuries governed by a prioress of gentle birth, they toiled in their orchards, wept, grew old and died.

Dr Frane's mild contempt for the unworldly life was evident, though he begged the Irishman's pardon if he gave any offense, for he had some very good friends who were Roman Catholic, very decent people. To which Ned Donovan replied that he had been brought up in the Anglican communion as thoroughly as had Dr Frane himself, his father having been butler to the Bishop of Clare, and no offense taken at all.

When Susan's face opened in astonishment, he grinned back and said: "Did I fail to mention?"

The convent being cloistered, the nuns could not go elsewhere to hear Mass, and no man could be permitted to live with them. So from very early on, when they rang their solitary bell upon a Sunday or holy day, one of the priestly monks trudged across the valley to hear their confessions and celebrate the Mass.

"By the year of Our Lord 1123 this serviceable priest had become known in the annals as the Prior of St Audrey, though you understand, that title was improperly assigned, or perhaps given in mockery. The priory being a convent of women was governed by a Lady Prioress. But, be that as it may, some chroniclers also call this monk by the name Conrad de Minton."

"Which one, the first one?"

"No, no, every one. The ecclesiastical histories report no other name for the so-called Prior, right up to the Abbey's dissolution under King Henry the Eighth."

"But that's impossible!"

The vicar shrugged lightly. "It is seldom commented upon in any of the sources I have examined. Thus I reckon it was believed or was indeed the same name with each incumbent."

Hands shaking, Miss Pickering set down her empty cup and broke off a bit of lemon scone to nibble at. The restlessness, wild magic, and lack of sleep had begun to take their toll.

"Do you mean to say," she wondered, "it was the same man?"

"My dear," Donovan said, then caught himself. "My dear, ehm, vicar. Are you saying this Conrad de Minton was immortal. An angel, maybe, or a demon?"

The name pronounced aloud a second time, the room darkened slightly. A passing cloud, surely, as the stormy sky grew closer.

"Oh, I think not. Not at the beginning, at any rate. A mortal man as much as you or I, though perhaps more cunning. There are a few tales. Mr Donovan, behind you there in the third shelf you'll find four volumes of the Annals of Philemon. In the second one, the chronicler makes that declaration most piously indeed. Further on he expresses some doubt, proposing that it might have been St Cuthbert himself, though that is quite ridiculous. Cuthbert, as you know, was associated with the North—Lindisfarne and Saint Columbanus, and thus—"

Ned Donovan cleared his throat. The vicar could take a hint, if not always hold onto it.

"Quite right, not important. But either their information was incomplete or it may have been—"

"Suppressed?" Ned supplied, sensing hesitation. "But why?"

Silently, the vicar hands lifted in a shrug. "A ghost, perhaps?"

"Forgive me, Vicar" said Susan, interrupting irritably. "Our spectral visitor is assuredly no saint, and no angel would be so vile. But surely a man must die before he can haunt anything. What is he?"

As her derision stretched into a yawn, Ned completed her thought. "I expect it is no more than a legend that grew in the telling of it. Generations of nuns, visited by a series of anonymous priests, simply copied the same name from one year to the next, and no one the wiser."

"A diary kept by a later Prioress calls him by that name, and names him a demon."

"That only proves he was a man," said Susan Pickering.

"You are becoming cynical, my child."

"I am exhausted, haunted, and beset by phantoms. Pray forgive me, and continue."

"This Conrad de Minton," the Irishman began.

A sharp shock rocked the room, and set the floor to rumbling. The second volume of Philemon came off the shelf and flew across the room. The tea tray and all its contents—cups, spoons, teapot and creamer—jumped and rattled as if the whole house shook in an earthquake. Lumps of sugar leapt from their bowl to splash into the cream. Tea fountained from the spout, showering the ancient tome on the desk just as the vicar shouted "Bless my soul!" and snatched it away.

The shaking stopped, and seconds later the teapot ceased spinning and toppled to the floor.

The vicar stared; they all stared for the length of an uncomfortable laugh.

"Bless my soul, indeed," the vicar breathed.

"Gracious!" said Susan, masking the rather stronger language from the reporter. Ned, in fact, uncorked his pocket flask and tipped it with apologies into his cup. Dr Frane declined in favor of a glass of port which he drank off with the ease of long practice.

Out of habit, Susan took it upon herself to right the upended tea things while Ned collected fallen books while Dr Frane collected himself. Finally settled, he cleared his throat.

"Demon he may well have been, for Conrad—" Across the room, the glass front of a book shelf cracked. "Well, we'll not say that name again, shall we? He was certainly wicked enough by all accounts. And perhaps he became one, not content with being merely a base, corrupted, and very long-lived monk."

"How do you mean corrupted?"

For the first time, the vicar became distinctly uncomfortable with the subject matter. Glancing at the other man in the room, however, won him permission to continue.

"There is a document in the Archbishop of Canterbury's library, stained and blackened, all but impossible to read, which records a series of testimonials from some of the nuns. Much of it is wild, almost insane, but from what I have puzzled out, they claimed this unholy Prior had sealed his soul to the Devil for the privilege of seducing them. But when that was accomplished, and the Devil was about to snatch him away, he twisted the Devil's tail to make a far more terrible bargain, exchanging twenty years of debauchery on earth for every nun he corrupted. As long as the Roman Church flourished in England, and as long as weary parents provided a constant supply of troublesome girls and pious widows, his opportunities to extend that contract must have been nearly endless. There is some evidence of the monks of St Cuthbert's frequenting the place, and others as well."

"How ghastly!" Susan had gone quite pale.

"From the commentaries of Berthold the Scrivener we know that this went on for a very long time. The families and even his superiors in the Church were fooled, you see, by the charm of the handsome Prior, as they thought of him. And so, supported by one worldly Prioress after another, he recruited women one by one into the dark pleasures and torments of that place. They say that those who resisted were slaughtered in terrible rituals."

"So they were, what? They were witches?"

"Of the worst sort. Devil worshippers," the vicar hissed. "Black magic and lustful—that is to say, carnal—oh dear!"

"You, Mr Donovan, as a man of the world, can perhaps imagine what it was like, though I certainly hope you cannot, Miss Pickering. Nasty rituals by the dark of the moon, indulging in all manner of vice until it was no more than a bawdy house. 'Making of God a cuckold' the bishop said when he read the anathema."

Eyes growing wider, Susan's heart was racing as a crimson blush swarmed up from the collar of her dress to bury itself in her bonnet. The voices, the lewd teasing, were not merely her too vivid imagination. All were real, and had happened before.

Donovan came and took her hands to calm her, propriety be damned.

"I suppose some clever novice finally did him in?" he said.

"The last mention of the so-called Prior of St Audrey is an undated letter from the Abbot of St Cuthbert's thanking the

Bishop for exorcising the beast, as he called him, and blessing the King in the person of his servant, Sir John Russell, for throwing down the convent and scattering the stones, so to speak. He also offered prayers for His Excellency's swift recovery from the bites and scratches delivered by the many familiar cats inhabiting the place. And for the souls of the women, too, although they were surely in hell, as he supposed."

"What happened to them, the nuns?"

"We can never be certain. The records are muddled, and of those that once existed, many were destroyed either at the time or under the tyrant Cromwell. Those days were so fraught with superstition and hysteria.

"Whatever that good bishop did, it seems to have worked, for we are told that on the very next day, the most powerful windstorm in a century swept through the Thames Valley. It uprooted the ancient hedges that used to preserve the convent from prying eyes, and threw down the orchards. Then the earth beneath opened up and all present were swallowed straight down into Hell itself. They say the flames were so hot they were only extinguished when the River Effra, by God's grace, rose from its banks and poured over the fire until it steamed away, which is why the river now is little more than a trickle in a meadow and a few brackish wells. And the name of De Minton was heard no more thereafter."

The disgusted sigh came from the young woman who had lived in that house nearly all her life. "If the whole convent was sucked into hell, how can my house have been built on its foundations?"

Donovan barked a short sharp laugh. "Good question, Miss Pickering. What really happened, sir?" he asked lightly. "It is clear the stories have got muddled: anathema, dissolution, conflagration? This is how myths begin, as my editor is fond of saying."

Dr Frane, who had been very mysterious throughout, relaxed and nodded his agreement. "They do say a legend has a grain of truth in it, but what that grain is, who can say now?"

"You've read so widely," the reporter smiled, "surely you have an idea. Was he hanged, do you think, this misbegotten priest, or burnt for witchcraft? Or did he swallow cold poison and jump in the sea?"

The old man chortled, laying his spectacles on the open book in front of him. "I believe the truth is that the anathema was spoken, the nuns dismissed, and the Prioress bound over for operating an unlicensed bawdy house. (I do beg your pardon, my dear.) The law was very hard on women in those days. The property was granted to Sir John Russell. Of the so-called Prior of St Audrey there is no final word except—"

He paused, steepling his fingers. Then suddenly he rose and went to the bell pull to call a servant. "Bless me, how the cold clutches at my bones nowadays."

"No final word, sir?" Donovan encouraged, feeling a sudden draft himself.

"Oh yes, well, there is a passage in *A History of Dilways and Shippenham*, of which we have only an incomplete copy, which mentions his being burnt at the stake, and his grimoire—that is his book of spells—buried along with other tools of his infamy. Afterwards, the, hmm, the ashes being gathered were, they were—" He rubbed a hand over each temple, pressing at a headache.

"I do not know. I fear that," he said, closing the ancient book, "is the sum of my knowledge and the limit of my speculation."

Susan had been listening all the while, alternately bewildered and pensive, and growing colder with each passing word.

"And what, pray, has all of that to do with Hollytree House?"

"My dear child, that house Gideon Pickering brought your mother to on that stormy night twenty-six years ago, the very night you were born, had been raised on those unhallowed grounds."

"I do not understand."

"I can say no more without violating your request for privacy, except this. There is a terrible curse connected with the property."

"A curse!" said Donovan. "Splendid!"

"Edward, please. It's nonsense."

"Is it, love? It may explain everything."

"It may indeed," the vicar went on, "for they say that from the midst of the flames, the mad prior spoke a most terrible curse. The words themselves are lost, but— Wait. Let me see."

Susan heaved a sigh, impatient with fairy tales.

While the vicar returned to the book and peeled back the pages, a maid with a coal scuttle entered, bundled in a shawl, and without even waiting for instructions began to poke up the fire in the little hearth. The whole house must have gone as cold as this room, though the addition of fuel did little to warm it.

"Ah, here it is, yes. *From the stake he demanded his grimoire be put into his hands instead of the Holy Scripture he had spurned. When the bishop naturally refused, the false prior screamed that in every generation he would return and claim a maiden as his tithe to hell, that he might never die. The curse would not be lifted until the evil book was returned to him or destroyed.*"

Susan, flinching from the images conjured by the words, stared down at her unremarkable hands to find she had been crumbling a scone into powder over her lap. When she exhaled, streamers of mist curled into the air.

The tension that had been mounting swallowed the room. Something tugged at her shawl, snatched away her bonnet, then goblin fingers seized her hands.

"Stop it!" Susan patted them away, almost in tears. "Stop it, all of you!"

She could not object when Donovan folded her into his arms, tucking her head protectively under his shoulder with soothing sounds that might even have been prayers. When a little figure of St Bartholomew with his tanner's knife arrowed towards them,

Donovan's hand shot out and slapped it aside. The music of tinkling glass told him it had broken a window.

"Leave this house! Be gone!!" cried the vicar, but he had no holy water, no tools but prayer, no procedures for this kind of thing.

The third volume of Philemon's *Annals* slipped from its place and flew across the room to clip him on the ear where he stood shouting the Lord's Prayer.

Dr Frane stared about in horror as ancient books and framed pictures danced about the room, crisp linen covers and crewel worked antimacassars took to the air and flew into the fire with a roar. More books joined the maelstrom.

The maid screamed, huddling in a corner and the vicar joined her.

"Begging your pardon, vicar," Donovan said, hardly raising his voice, "but I believe we'll be going. You've been very helpful."

As at the stationers, silence fell in their wake. Though the hour was no more than eight of a long summer evening, storm clouds blackened the sky hurrying the night before them. A thick fog had risen from the river, wedding with the woodland mists. Before they could go further than the Greyhound, rain had begun falling in earnest out of a sable sky. They would be a while getting home.

When at last they straggled in, even the maids had stumbled to their beds, and Mrs Knox's muttering had declined into a gentle snore. Ned didn't like the thought of his beloved going to her rooms alone, and she would not have him sleeping outside her door. So with quiet murmurs and the occasional sneeze they went about the old house together and checked the locks, rattled doors and windows, peered into closets in unoccupied rooms, until they were satisfied. Only the usual snuffling and snores, and light murmuring from the Haliwell's rooms, disturbed the peace of the house in the slightest.

Still restless, they sat up playing Hearts and listening to the timbers creak until after midnight. At no time did Susan volunteer to share the family secrets so intently hinted at, not even when pressed.

By the time she fell exhausted into her own bed, no ghoul nor ghost nor long-legged beastie had any hope of disturbing her sleep.

VI
Alliance

AGAIN, MR DONOVAN was not at breakfast. Miss Pickering informed the others of the funeral plans, then enquired whether there had been any further troublesome experiences during the night. Which answer came in the form of nervous laughter and the quick scraping back of chairs. Hats on, bonnets secured, box lunches collected, and they had gone. Troubled dreams, she guessed, but nothing more. When she glanced at old Mr Haliwell, his childlike smile warmed the creased parchment of his features, then he too left the table.

Apart from interviewing a pair of blushing newlyweds in search of modestly priced but respectable lodgings, she had little to do with her day but grieve, and worry and wait for the night and the Prior's next move. Then she remembered it was market day in Sydenham Wells, and her stipend had arrived. So she popped on her bonnet and shawl, and with Peter and a large basket went out into the rain-fresh day.

In the afternoon, Donovan found Susan in the garden, combing out her hair and staring up at the sky. The long damp locks smelled of steam and French soap, and the color she hated glinted in the sun with tips of gold. Never having been privileged to see it at its full length before, he almost turned and left, but couldn't.

"My goodness, ma'am," he said, daring to take the comb from her hand. She startled at first touch, then relaxed as the smooth downward motion continued. He sensed her rare smile and longed to see it, but this liberty was not to be wasted.

"When I came outside, I thought one of Her Majesty's younger daughters had stopped in to visit, so I did."

"Very courtly, sir," she answered graciously. "And very kind though I think you must need eye glasses."

"Pray do not question my taste in beauty," he said. Returned the comb then calmly separated her hair into three sections and braided the length of it with surprising skill, then handed the end to her over one shoulder. While she examined what she could see of it for flaws, he pulled a length of string from a pocket and proceeded to neatly bind the end.

"Very tidy, Mr Donovan. Have you been a sailor?"

"I've been many things, *mo croí*. And now I am looped in the loops of your hair."

"Such liberties, Mr Donovan," said Susan. After a moment in which she thought she might well faint, she said: "I suppose I shall have to marry you now."

"I beg your pardon, my dear Miss Pickering. Is that a yes?"

So many possibilities. So many things that needed saying before that final assent.

Since returning from the market, Susan had been at her writing desk much of the afternoon reading through the papers from her grandmother's solicitors and shaking her head. The duchess never communicated directly. Probably for the best. That snobbish old lady would not be amused to find her granddaughter betrothed to an Irishman, no matter what his religion. What she would do if they actually married did not bear thinking of.

Taking a deep breath, she met the grey eyes directly and said: "Let us be rid of this ghost, or demon, or whatever it is. Then you may ask me properly."

"And you'll explain what the vicar meant?"

"And all the rest. Although, when I have, you may wish to reconsider."

"I never will," he said framing her flushed face between his ink-stained hands. "You are my own heart."

The wide eyes blinked as he pressed a kiss above them and felt, with her, the surge of the nameless gift they shared: to hear the bells of Elfland, as Mr Fitzroy had called it.

"Oh my!" she exclaimed softly.

"Oh, yes," he answered, moving his lips to hers. They would need it more than churches, that gift.

The moment lengthened while she kissed him back, trembling with the magic that always astonished her. Until the shuffling sound of hard boots on gravel threw them apart, Ned Donovan jumping to his feet.

He cleared his throat: "Have they finished with the garden yet?" he said, a bit more loudly than necessary

"What?" Susan let go of a dreamy smile, already accustomed to the reporter's sudden shifts of attention. "Not yet. Why?"

A few days earlier, at her request, Ned had brought in a crew to tear out the neglected flower beds and make a proper kitchen garden as she'd long intended. She'd been listening to their echoes all day, the scrape of spades and barrows rumbling. Now one of them seemed to be coming up to the house

"Those lads we hired. I asked them to keep an eye out for anything unusual, especially around the garden walls and that old fountain at the back. Ah, and so they must have done!"

Leaving Susan astonished, he dashed into the house and in a moment, was in the parlour. Slipping the locks on one set of French doors, he flung them open. Fresh air swept into the stuffy parlour along with the sunshine. Susan dashed into the room to save the papers fluttering on her desk.

Donovan shouted, "You, there! Yes, indeed. Bring that over here, if you please!"

A few words with the foreign workman and the workman's young nephew, whose English was better, and Ned turned to Susan with an excited grin twisting up his fiery whiskers. In his arms he carried an ancient iron-bound box the size of a small child, with dried muck and white worms' ends flaking onto the faded Turkey carpet.

"As I thought. They planted the fountain over it. And isn't it grand!" he announced cheerfully. "Bit of a mess, but—"

"Stop right there!" Susan protested, horrified. "Edward Francis Donovan, do not take another step with that thing!"

The linen dresser stood just in the hall, and she knew at least one sheet that had more than served its time. She'd patched it again last week, with Daisy's help.

Oh, dear Daisy! Daisy, who always kicked the cupboard closed even though it meant having to clean the smudge her boot left behind. The smudge which, startled, Susan saw there now.

Nonsense, she thought, as she dug in the back of the cupboard. The smudge had already slipped her mind by the time she returned with the sheet, Peter, a broom and a pan, just seconds too late. Of course the ridiculous man had paid no attention and dropped the filthy box on the table, sacrificing a painted souvenir plate from the Crystal Palace and a potted African violet.

At Susan's look, he heaved it up again and let Peter snatched off the fringed shawl so she could lay the old sheet in its place. Then they both stepped back while Peter cleared away the wreckage.

A wooden box two foot long, ten inches on the square, with the wood grain stained dark with age and earth, it must have been a handsome piece of work once. Bound with blackened metal bands, the sides and top were carved with scrolling vines inlaid with metal wire all but consumed by tarnish. A few tendrils retained a glint of gold or brass where the light fell on them, but dirt and some hard white stuff filled in the rest.

Donovan dragged a pair of chairs back to the table for them both to sit and ponder the thing. On a hasp at the front, a thick iron barrel the size of his fist appeared to be the lock. There would be no key, of course, but you could tell that any key would be useless. The keyhole itself was clogged, caked with dried, nameless filth.

"Is that blood?"

"Of course not."

Chin propped on one hand, he reconsidered the lie, then sent Peter for a hammer and chisel. "Well, now, I'm afraid it probably is."

The boy dashed back into the room, bearing tools and begging leave to have a go.

"Best not, lad." Jacket off, shirt sleeves rolled. "My new friend at the British Museum won't take well to my smashing a 300-year-old artifact—when it's time to tell him. But the Museum are used to being cross with me."

Two good blows and the brittle iron lock lay in pieces on the linen.

"Blimey!" said Peter.

Susan sent the boy away with orders to close the door behind him and stand watch.

Laying big freckled hands on either side of the domed lid, Donovan met only resistance and a splinter as he tried to shift it. And one other thing. A tingling, maybe; a vibration in the palms of his hands where they laid against the wood.

Whether frozen by magic or only swollen by the ordinary actions of time and damp, the lid refused to budge, There was no telling what might be harmed if he simply bashed in the lid, so he took up the chisel again. Setting it against the seam, he gave it a tap every few inches.

Between taps, he explained. "I had a word with Joseph, he's the chief of the men we hired, speaks excellent English. Used to work the digs for ferenji archaeologists in Mesopotamia. Henry Layard, and that lot."

"You said they were gardeners."

Tools down. A held breath and a new grip around the box. No movement, just brown and grey muck streaking his tweed waistcoat.

"No, *a ghrá*, I said they were labourers. This lot may not know a rose from a radish, but they do know better than to throw anything like this on the rubbish heap without letting their gov'nor have a look."

"You don't think it's anything to do with the prior's curse, do you?"

"No idea," he grinned. "We only learnt about that yesterday. It could be Roman coins or Viking plunder. Maybe just a box of mouldy old hymnals, eh?"

Susan scoffed delicately. "If there'd been a treasure buried in the garden, I'm sure my father would have found it long ago. And spread it all round the East End, God rest his great heart."

"I thought your father was a solicitor?"

"So he was, but not the sort you're familiar with. How did you know that?"

"Research," Donovan wheezed, tapping a bit harder, "remember? History of the house and its owners?"

"Investigating the vast tracts of land you'll come into when we marry?" Her wry question was only half in jest.

"Of course," he chuckled. "As I'm marrying a propertied woman, my lawyers will insist."

He went quiet, then, just as she had, realizing how that must sound when he had only meant to tease her. Uncomfortable, he cleared his throat and turned back to the box.

"If I had any lawyers, that is. Right, well, you'd best stand away. One more thing to try."

Turning the box back-to-front, he hefted the hammer and gave a pair of great whacks to the iron hinges, then held his breath as the lid wrenched free with a squeal of tortured wood. A cloud of dust and fine ash swirled up behind it reeking of burnt honey, meadow flowers, and sweet hay that covered something sour.

Susan jumped back, blinking behind her glasses, and waved away the dust with annoyance and a flapping apron. A peculiar look twisted Donovan's face, once he'd stopped sneezing.

"What the devil?"

Meeting Susan's wide brown eyes, he held out his hand and after a moment's hesitation, she took it. Together they peered into the casket. No Viking gold nor jeweler's hoard, nor any other obvious treasure, not even hymnals. It looked to be half-filled with a mixture of fine earth and coarse grey dust. Layered within lay bags and pouches of all sizes: some of leather, some cloth of gold, some silk-embroidered, and each drawn closed with a discoloured cord.

On top of all lay a sheet of parchment that might have been a list, but the antiquated Latin and crabbed medieval hand defeated Donovan's quick glance.

"Catalog," he coughed, and set it aside. "The contents, maybe. Anyway, the vicar will want that."

Cautious, he reached in to bring out the top-most bag, and opened it.

Susan didn't mean to squeak when the bone appeared, but even the most sensible woman can be taken by surprise. The quick breath caked her throat with floating filth as the thing slid out of the bag, clean and polished as old ivory.

"A long leg bone, I think," Donovan suggested while Susan coughed. "Is that the femur or the other one?"

He poked a finger around the contents of a small round bag like a gambler's dicing pouch. "Not the usual knucklebones. I think these are the bones of a child's hand. Saint Hugh, maybe. Or so they would tell you. Look there is marked III. The Roman number 3, that would be. I wonder why?"

Sensible Susan had no more squeaks in her though a cold hand clutched her heart, and she had begun to feel queasy.

"But why? Who would do this?"

"Holy relics," he concluded with more disdain than piety. "All decorated and neatly numbered for the catalog. All buried in the midden to stop mad old King Henry the Eighth throwing them on the fire, I imagine. Or the wicked prior. Look here, this one's very old, enameled in four colours. Maybe it is St Audrey's patella worn out from kneeling. And this would be..."

Light as Flemish lace, a tiny skull came clean and white into his hand. "...St Audrey's cat?"

"A holy familiar?"

"Good as gold to the priory for the pilgrim fees alone— when they still welcomed pilgrims."

"Well," Susan said, "it was a treasure to someone, I'm sure, but hardly gold in great store to us now. I expect the vicar will want to put them on display. Is there nothing but bones?"

. "Here's something odd." Hands sunk into the dusty matrix, he pulled out and knocked the dust off a long thin bag, dove gray though the folds showed it had once been deep blue. It proved to contain a length of pale wood stripped and burnished, banded in gold and smelling faintly of incense. Even with the metalwork, it weighed almost nothing. It was also un-numbered. Frowning, Donovan laid it aside with the rest.

Next to appear, a leather envelope holding folded papers, the ink smeared, layers glued together by time and damp.

"Proceedings, I suppose, the priory charter, the letter of dissolution. The vicar will be delighted to have the complete record."

"You really have no shame."

"I know. And yet, you love me still," he said.

"So you keep telling me."

"Will you fetch a pencil, *a ghrá*, and your drawing pad? If we are good archaeologists, we should have drawings as good as yours. With your fine eye for detail, who knows, we might learn something useful."

"The— the magic never shows past things, you know," she murmured, "only the passing moment."

"Oh, yes, right you are." He held up another item, heavy and angular in a rust-red bag, stiff and stained with black. "This would be a book. And more blood I think. Hmm."

"A book?"

Despite his care, plush silk threads parted over a plain leather cover gone green with age, scorched and smelling of the flame.

"Breviary, maybe, or a book of hours?"

She had not thought her heart could sink any further. "Or maybe the wicked prior's book of evil spells? The grimoire." Susan took it from him while he carried on his explorations. "I think we've found it. We've found him."

He paused, and they both peered into the box, then at all the relics already discovered.

"What is all that dust, or ash? Edward, what happens to a body when it's burnt at the stake? We say 'dust to dust' but is it that, or is it ash and shattered bones?"

"Shall I tell you, little wren?" said the voice in her mind, brittle as ice. *"Release me, and you shall know."*

"Now that is something I do not know," he admitted. The relics were buried in a loose mixture of earth and something else: dirty ash with black bits, grey flakes and charred bits of white bone, so thin they collapsed under his touch.

I suppose I should have put a handkerchief over my nose.

"And you are in it to the elbows!"

"Mmm."

The reporter, who had seen more than a few terrible things from shipwreck to charnel house, seemed scarcely to notice as Susan backed away.

Near the garden doors a marred writing desk stood at the entrance to the palm-shaded alcove, bathed in summer light. Turning the key, she lowered the cover to release a clutter of crumpled paper, a broken pen, the angry letter she'd abandoned for the solace of a bath—and that was a measure of her distress. Above the mess, half a dozen tidy pigeonholes each housed some part of her life: her book of accounts, legal documents, accounts to be paid.

On the shelf above, two miniature portraits in a single frame, her parents gazed at each other as if their love were all that mattered in the world. As a girl, Susan had often wished they would turn away, just once, to look at her. Now, just for a moment, she imagined that this time, they might, there was that much magic loose in the room. She could hear it ringing in her ears.

She meant to sit. No, first she meant to collect the new sketch book from the Bremerton's box with an alarming number of items in it. She meant to apply her good sense and set to documenting their find. Instead she stood transfixed, sloughing away the remains of the book's silk wrapper.

"Yes, open it. Read it!"

Susan shrugged away the voice, determined not to listen. It felt at first simply old: long buried, long decayed, smelling of mildew and must that wrinkled her nose, but weighed down with incense, fear, and black magic. Slowly, she tipped the cover open with one finger, peeled back the first foxed pages to read the strange Gothic hand. English, yes, though the characters had a foreign look, some spiked and looped, some underscored, others stained red and brown.

Her stomach knotted as she read rhymed couplets describing in fine detail and execrable verse the habits of the prior and his so-called nuns. Foul language and vile practices inhabited the charms he used to hold them; speaking them aloud made them hum with life. Worse still in their way were the clean, businesslike agreements detailing the terms by which this mad priest, the string of Prioresses, girl after lost girl cast away their souls. Each agreement subscribed in what Susan knew instinctively was blood.

Diagrams and drawings in arcane symbols delineating with demonic pride a history of seduction, debauchery, and riot fed by blood and twisted magic. Horned imps and winged monkeys looked on with leering delight, left her ignorant of no detail.

The pages turned almost of themselves as she stood, frozen to the spot. The cold voice, almost musical, seemed to be reading them to her, tireless, seductive, and vile.

Her gorge rose with each new page. And yet she could not stop nor move to put it down until the last page crumbled.

"All the powers of the world shall be yours, Susannah. Come be my prioress, my queen."

"No, no!" she demanded. "Ned!"

"What's that, love?" said he, hearing some distress, but when he glanced up, he saw her standing still with the prior's book open in her hand, her face the blank mask of the intent reader.

"Spells. Disgusting." The words caught in her throat.

"Set it down then," Ned said, making his own mental notes. "We shall look at it later together. Are you all right?"

Something stirred the air, the parchment list on the table caught his eye, and he turned to it.

An errant breeze slipped through the gaps of the tall doors, eddying along the walls and floor. It caught at her hair, teasing out damp curls to frame her face. The long braid so lovingly plaited swiftly uncoiled to let the hair ripple shining past her waist.

It snatched the breath from her mouth, and blanketed her in cold. Chilled to stillness, even time seemed to have stopped: No sound came from the table where Ned was so earnestly engaged. Flames in the hearth hovered over the coals like a painting of fire. No breath curled from her mouth. Only the words, the incessant voice in her mind, directed, cajoled, implored her attention.

A rumbling disturbed the silence, and a flicker of shadow. Had Edward said her name? When she turned, or thought she turned, she could barely see him, as if the room had swallowed him. Alone with the demon, the ghost, the prior of St Audrey, fear numbed her mind.

"Look, Susannah, see who is here."

Against her will she looked where she was told. Beyond the French doors, distorted by the warped glass of the old windows, where the overgrown flower garden should be stood neat rows of cherry trees. Row after row of cherry trees marched through scythed lawns right up to the house, clouding the sky with their crowns of white blossom.

What has happened? she wondered. A moment later, she had forgotten the question.

"Susannah!" A honeyed breath fraught with promise caressed her ear. "I have made it all for thee."

"You know my name." She could almost see him

"I have always known you, child. When that willful girl eloped with her solicitor, I rose to sing her an aubade."

"No. You are lying."

"I was here for your first wobbling steps, when you broke your crown on the piano bench. The blood you shed was spilt for me."

"It was not, stop saying that. Let me go."

"I was here when the old harridan, your Grandmama, came to take you from this house. I tasted your tears. When you were gone, I slept."

"This is impossible."

"I am here for you now, Susannah. Come lie with me! Rest! No mouldering house demands your time and money. No servants skulking or guests ungrateful. No family both rejecting and demanding. Only peace, and freedom."

How did he know anything about her family? Though the marriage had been irregular, it was an honest one. The duchess would not have it colored with scandal, or leave herself open to rebuke for neglecting poor Amelia's child. And so when Susan was sixteen, Grandmama had come to the Hollytree in person to collect her over Gideon's strong objections. Then for three years she had lived with the Duchess and Cousin Gwendolyn and Great Uncle Erasmus, and a houseful of sneering servants, and she had crumbled under their condescension and their scorn.

Poor, mousey, unremarkable Susan had been given two or three handsome but very plain gowns for her Season, along with dancing lessons and some instruction in how to comport herself in Society. Her season, like all her other years, had at all times suffered by comparison with the glittering, giggling Gwendolyn, surrounded by wealthy boys just as shallow as she.

Then Susan failed to marry, as if that had ever been a question, once the whispers began. Her father was a Jew, they said. Or his mother was, and a foreign Jewess, at that. It explained why so much of his practice was among the poor of the East End: Jews and Irish, even Lascars and Chinese. If Susan was not a bastard, still she was certainly no catch.

These were her secrets. These the stories she had not yet given the man she loved. Better to keep them and his friendship than let the truth drive him away.

The brows knitted into a frown. "What are you?"

"Does it matter? Put down your cares, Susannah. Step into the garden with me. Bring my book to me there. Tell me your secrets, and your apostle I shall be."

"Stop!"

"Hush. Say nothing only grant me this boon."

She was so weary, and the book so heavy. Grief bore her down. And how could she resist the beautiful voice, deep and loving as an angel, speaking only to her. Her eyelids drifted closed against the brilliant light. Yes, yes she would go into the cherry orchard.

Susan nodded. "I must tell Edward," she said, or maybe she did not.

"He will not come," the soothing voice corrected. "He is not here. He died at the railway station."

"Did he? No, I saved him."

"He did not love you. Come to me and be loved."

What did he want from her? Oh yes, the book. She was holding an old book that shone in the darkness like a flame. Why should she fight at all? Why not be warm instead of cold; why not accept and rest? Rest. Her mind was weary as her limbs, and her heart. She hardly knew what she thought.

No! Susan tried to stamp her foot. No, she would not join him. Her heart lay here, not in impossible landscapes. Where was love but in this house? She was not alone, though she resisted taking the final steps.

And yet, strange music drew her, and beneath it, a low insistent cadence like a drum, no, a heartbeat at odds with her own. It sang to her of another world beyond the door, a softer world without worry or work or accounts to pay, without a family disgraced by her mere existence. A world where virtuous nuns paced a shadowed path among the trees, their praying hands clasped at hidden breasts. There they were now, so peaceful!

"Look, Susannah! Do you not see her?" the voice whispered. "Your mother is among them. Go to her. A mother's love is all you need."

So the libertine, the monster, had come to it after all. "No" she whimpered, though her lips barely moved. "No, my mother is gone."

"She is here, You have but to look."

Among the procession, all veiled nuns, the tallest of the grey women turned her head slightly. Two lights within the concealing wimple shone out like candle flames in silvered mirrors, then withdrew. More figures trailed after her into a hazy vine-covered wall, into peace unending.

Why were some of them giggling? Were they the mischievous singers of the night before? The mocking, lascivious ones who would have her for their sister.

"Open the door. She waits for thee, and thy sisters also."

"No," she murmured, fighting him in earnest now.

"Liar! That is not my mother. They are dead. All of them, long dead, because of me. I must find Edward."

"What is Edward? There is no Edward."

"Edward is . . ." the cold grabbed at her mind. A name, just a name, a question, another fear. He was . . . intimate, improper. So much power in a name. So much to lose if she married. Edward! The fury flickered again,

Confused, she swayed in place as she batted feebly at the invisible hands plucking at her clothes. She was so cold.

"You must open the door. Take the book into the cloister. We will go together to thy mother and she will read to us of love, and I will wed you, Susannah. I will teach you every delight."

Weary of clinging to a insubstantial image, she felt the voice more than heard it now: a tingle on her skin, insistent. A sweet voice but impatient. If only it would stop badgering, she could think.

Troubled, Susan watched the passing procession of grey ladies with their glittering eyes, longing to be one of them. The music called, and her lost sisters. She had only to open this door.

"Join them," said the smooth voice seductive in her ear. A cool suggestion of arms encircled her waist. "They are all your sisters. Sing with them among the lilies. Sport with them upon the rose petals, let them feed you upon apricocks and plums and cherries ripe and I shall love you all. Only open the door and join them. Take me my book, Susannah. Take it out of the house, and I shall come to you in the flesh!"

Uncertain still, her hand drifted toward the latch.

"Stop!"

She halted, the cold wall cracked, time reasserted itself around her, though sluggishly. "Edward?"

VII
Bound

STRANGE MUSIC ECHOED in Ned Donovan's mind driving out, finally, the dainty fa-la-las. Driving out and gradually snapping his intent fascination with the iron-bound casket. And with the tune, the awareness that the music was not meant for him. He straightened suddenly

"*A cuishla?*" said Donovan. "Susan, love, where are you going?"

He saw her poised before the French doors, clutching the grimoire; the other hand hovered over the curled iron latch. The high-necked bodice lay on the floor beside her, revealing a white bosom constrained by an embroidered corset. Her shift was slipping from shoulders mantled in her long brown hair, all his loving work undone. What he could see of her face, half turned from him, was wild: lips parted, eyes half-closed, the complexion two spots of high color in a face as white as death.

Donovan shivered, his pulse quickened. A thread of cold knotted up his vision, distorting the air, hiding her from him in a darkening haze. He blinked it away, shivering.

"Susan?" He started to move around the table, but was halted, as if a strong armed copper had put out a hand to keep him away. More urgently he cried, "Susan!".

In answer came a merry song, centuries old:

> *Brief is life, and brevity*
> *Briefly shall be ended:*

Harsh music jangled, pipes and tabors, tambourines, the reveling voices of Goliards drunken and licentious.

Death comes like a whirlwind strong,
Bears us with his blast along;
None shall be defended.

"What does that mean?" Donovan demanded "Answer me!"

The room filled up with the shades of riotous boys and girls, tonsured monks and crop-haired nuns riding their shoulders with their gowns kirtled up to their thighs. They circled Susan's motionless figure, laughing, teasing, plucking at her clothes.

This was the other side of magic, not the golden song of Faerie but deceit and malice, the love of power. Fearful understanding grew as he bent his mind toward Susan's, seeking their shared connection. Blinking, rubbing his eyes, he strove to see her through the haze that only grew thicker, as if the sun had died, the room and garden beyond drowned in night.

Ned swore in two languages, possibly three. Something batted his thought away, began to resolve into a lucent figure like a cowled monk. It hovered at Susan's side with one hand caressing her hair. All the while muttering words Donovan could almost make out, staring in fury.

Still, Ned thought, if the prior could simply take the woman, he would have done so. Perhaps it was not that easy. And if he needed only to pay his "tithe", then the maid Daisy must have filled that role. But they had disturbed his ashes, and they had found his book. Found it, and foolishly brought it while the creature still roamed the halls. But what if that were not his only desire? What if, once the book came again into his sphere—and if he could seduce an innocent into reading it aloud—the creature could manifest into the world again. The grimoire wherein his Master had inscribed a final charm.

In the seconds these possibilities took to form, Donovan's voice returned to him, and his control. Also the beginnings of a plan.

"You, Prior!" he snapped. The creature glanced up, the predatory eyes gleaming dull red. "This house is full of women. You took the little maid. Why?"

The image appeared to shrug. "The child wanted me! What could I do?"

"You seduced and tormented her for your master's sake. Now you do the same with my Susan, who wants no part of you. You've done enough harm!"

"Hey ho, no no! Without you be a unicorn, and I know you are not, she is not yours to claim!"

Chanting, dancing with Susan, he swung her about until she faced the Irishman with no expression in her eyes.

"She gave me a cherry withouten any stone, and a meekly dove without a bone. Heigh ho, my boy! Her cherry had no stone until I gave her mine, you see, ah ha!"

It was too hard to bear. "Stop it, you villain!"

"Can you make me, scribbler, dribbler, fibbler? Can you construe, contort, contrive, and swive? Oh, scrivener, art thou alive! Such boneless, bloodless anger is in you. If you want her you should have her. Heigh ho, the cherry, that is she, your melting mistress, cherry ripe and ripe for plucking, ah. But ah! Too late for you, too late!"

"Liar."

"I have been in her dreams night after night. In your guise she teaches me to pray between her thighs. My bone to her cherry, enfolded in the ripe flesh, red as coral, bursting..."

"Monster!"

Was it working? The prior's attention diverted to bragging left his control of Susan unattended while he taunted his rival

"Shall I tell you why she has never married? Already the bride of the Priory, I shall her make my Prioress, my voluptuous whore. When I have my book again, with all the spells at my command, I shall take her with full force, manifesting in the instant of her cataclysm."

"You mean her to die?"

"I mean to become a god!"

The reporter leapt forward only to find his body seized with cold. Every limb, shackled, weighted him down, preventing every motion. Only his senses remained.

The dancing monks and nuns, the prior himself, flickered and swirled, melting into a whirlwind. It threw off wisps of energy, bouncing like lightning in a jar, sparking at Susan's lips and hands. It lifted her skirts, flung up her arms, and whipped her hair around her throat like a scarf. But a light had begun to shine about her, the deep brown eyes glimmered, Ned thought, with tears as she fought back.

So much effort must be taking its toll on the wicked prior. Perhaps the prior had overreached his powers, or Susan herself was stronger than either of them had imagined.

And what if, Ned wondered, without the grimoire the creature's power was in fact no more than illusion and a smooth tongue. What if none of this was real?

Oh, it felt real enough, that he knew as he struggled again to free himself, to reach Susan, though it was like swimming in treacle. Fighting for each sliding step, he persisted in drawing attention to himself, away from his beloved.

"So it is you, then, Prior," Donovan said tightly. "As we guessed. Vile, proud, bathed in blood."

"Stupid man, you cannot insult me."

The voice came from everywhere, dripping with arrogance.

"Perhaps not, but I can defeat you. The bound casket is your coffin, isn't it, wrapped in its iron bands. The ashes are yours, buried with twelve holy relics to keep you down! The parchment I thought was a list or a catalog was nothing of the kind. It is the spell that keeps you bound."

"Yes! They burnt my body, bonnie and beautiful, they smashed my bones to dust. They brought down my convent with all its treasures, and hanged my luscious oh, my lovely girls."

"Your whores, you mean, that you defiled. The better to destroy them."

"Self-righteous, sanctimonious scribbler!" the prior snarled. "That canting fat bishop stole my grimoire and put it on the fire, but it did not burn. But you have found it, peasant. You have freed me!"

"Not yet, I think, or you would not need this woman. Is that why you killed the maid?"

Impatiently it sneered, "The milksop maid was of no use except to stir my lust, though she served to catch your notice."

"You are mad. You have been mad for a thousand years! What about Susan?"

"Blind, blind, blind as two bats you are!" the voice shrieked.

"No!" The swirling wind tightened around the girl. He could not let that happen. "No, I see well enough. You need your grimoire. The bishop could not burn it, but nor could he keep it safe from others of your sort. So he buried it in the same box, weighed down like yourself by sanctity and superstition."

"Still a fool. It is the woman's house. It was the woman's longing all unsatisfied that summoned me; her drawings that woke me. Such magic is nothing of my Master's. When I have consumed her power I shall dissolve my ancient bargain. Then shall I be free of Hell, and return unto the world once more, mine own master."

The shock burst out of Ned in mocking laughter. "Medieval idiot, you know nothing. True for you, the power is no devil's work, but nor is it in the woman. The spell is on the sketchbook, charmed by a lord of Faerie. 'Tis art alone lies in my girl's left hand, along with your book of spells, and I'll not let you have the one nor the other."

And therein lay the kernel of the plan. His ashes ground fine and mixed with earth, bound and buried, Conrad de Minton remained a spectre with no substance and no power to claim his grimoire from where the bishop had laid it. Only Susan Pickering, the heiress and mistress of the place, could return it to him, and she stood folded in enchantment like Cleopatra in her carpet. If only Donovan could find a way to unroll it.

Out of a hollow shout, a hot wild laughter echoed through the parlour, rattling every window. Shrieking, the wind swept pictures from the wall, jangled the harp strings, raked the courses of the pianoforte into a roar.

"Ridiculous mortal," the voice bellowed, stripped of its beauty. "Prating child! I could kill you with a thought, as easily as the simple-minded maid.

"But you haven't, yet, have you? You can do nothing without the woman."

"Fool, you will watch me as I take her."

The monk's image flashed about kissing Susan, stroking her flushed cheek, embracing her arched body, its cackling laughter bouncing off the walls on every side.

"No!" Ned shouted. "You will never do it!"

At least he had achieved a step forward; the roiling air faltered slightly. Irritated, the figure steadied itself behind Susan's shoulder and glared: a saturnine face smirking within a cowl, black eyes filled with malice above a curling beard. All his effort concentrated on breaking the spell that held him, Donovan hardly noticed Susan's hand rising toward the door.

Someone else was watching.

YOU MUST STOP HER! said a clear, light voice nearby, or perhaps in his mind alone. SHE MUST NOT TAKE THE BOOK TO HIM!

"That I know," Ned thought, then commanded: "Susan, come away from the door."

He slid his other foot forward, more easily this time. "Let go the book, and come away!"

In response to him, or to something else, who could say, her head began to turn over her shoulder until the face, her dear face, peered at him through the flying ribbons of her hair. Struck by her expression, Ned felt the gooseflesh rise along his arms. A more blank and empty expression he had never seen on a living creature, careless and cold with no color in it but black. His throat tightened as the chill invaded his chest.

Still he gasped, "Susan Pickering, for your soul's sake, you must come away!"

Beside her, the prior's ghost raised a furious hand.

"Be silent, fool. You cannot stay me."

The raised hand clenched and pounded the air. The evil will hammered against Donovan's heart with such a force it flung him back across the room to crash on the delicate table that held the iron-bound trunk. Screeching, the table gave way beneath him, and the bones and bags, ashes and graveyard dust raining about him.

"Well that's real enough," Ned Donovan gasped, shaking his head clear. But he had a will and a temper, too, and when he should have given way to despair, they raised him up. He might ache all over, but he could move freely again.

Head ringing, he struggled to his knees, senses alive with awareness of the bits and bones scattered around him. The Prior might still have some magic, but the old Bishop that finally bound him had known a thing or two. Everything in the box was there for a reason, he knew that. But what, and how could they serve him now? How could he divine their purpose in the instants that remained?

"Help me," he hissed to his imaginary friend, "whoever you are."

CALL ME GRIFFIN. EVERYTHING YOU NEED IS UNDER YOUR HAND. I WILL AID YOU IF I CAN.

Freezing fingers touched each one, hurriedly examining and setting it aside until he knelt within a circle of relics in which he had no faith and little understanding. Well, that didn't matter either, if only he could divine their purpose. What would his Granny Gillain do?

TICK TOCK, MY SON. OUR MINUTES HASTEN TO THEIR END.

Minutes. The clock was ticking. The box was a coffin. A coffin, and a reliquary. Each piece in the box had been catalogued and numbered. The parchment. What had happened to the parchment? In his pocket, of course. But when he fetched it out, the words swam before him. Hopeless.

MIND YOUR HEAD, THE FAERY SAID—CAN YOU READ?

A spark grew warm between his ruddy brows. Donovan rubbed his eyes, blinked, and remembered the bluebell faery in the wood. He looked again and the spiky letters swarmed into words that made sense.

> *St Martin's thigh bone: I.*
> *Feather from St Cuthbert's raven: II.*
> *The Hildelith patella, enameled: III.*
> *The knuckle bones of Saint Swithbert the Younger: IV.*

Twelve in all, like the hours of the day, or the face of a clock. It was not a list, it was the binding spell itself.

Still on his knees Donovan rescued each piece, hastily seeking and finding the Roman numerals. Gradually he could feel the air change, gathering warmth and lightness as he slid each one into its designated place; sense an energy gathering within him until the last relic clicked audibly into place. The air above the ring began to hum. Now what?

Something nudged his left hand, his working hand, until he lifted it and found the polished, un-numbered hazel wand with its bands of gold. In wonder, he curled his fingers around it and felt the magic singing in his blood.

YES! his helper said.

The right hand reached on its own for the fragile skull, inked with swirls and a few careful characters—a word in Greek. Hopefully, he didn't have to pronounce it, only tap into its power.

BLESSINGS ON YOU, HUMAN CHILD.

Donovan opened his mind, drew a long breath, waiting.

Now call to her. Call her by her proper name.

Her proper name? Donovan frowned, hating the delay. Then the memory found him.

Yesterday's post, arriving on the rare day when he happened to be at home. A fat packet from a pair of fat solicitors with Susan's full legal name flowering across the envelope. He'd made a joke then thought no more about it, but that's all right. He remembered now.

Another flicker, the monkish figure raced toward him, halting barely an arm's length away, arrested by the perimeter of saintly bones.

"What are you doing?" the hollow voice demanded.

"Taking her from you."

"Go to, boy. You do not command here!"

"I do not," Donovan said gravely, nodding toward his beloved. "But she does."

Elsewhere in Hollytree House, a copper dinner gong broke the air. From across the hillside six brazen notes pealed the hour from St Barnabas' sharp new steeple. A light breeze from somewhere brushed the strings of the tall harp in the corner.

Rising on his painful knees Ned thrust the wand towards his beloved with a strong hand and shouted:

"Susannah Adele, Gideon's daughter, I tell you by the love we share, come away from that door!"

Lightning found him. Electricity sizzled down his arm and blasted from the hazel wand, enclosing Susan and the grimoire in a bubble of iridescent light. The wind died at once. Her head snapped around, eyes blazing through the fall of all her rippling hair. She blinked twice. The spell like melting ice fell away from her in grey shards, and she thrust out her hand to her lover.

Breathless, she cried, "Edward! Lend me your strength!"

"A free gift it is, *a cuishla mo chroí!*" he called, and flung what he had to her along the length of his arm, directing it through the hazel shaft.

A silver bell sounded in the air.

"What's this, boy? You have given away what little magic you could squeeze from dust and bone and sealing wax. Like the last wash through the honeycomb, that is but weak mead."

The hollow voice creaked with scorn, unfaltering. "And to a woman. Ha! Long hair, short wit!"

"Conrad de Minton!" Susan's voice rang out rich and low, a bronze bell tolling. "In God's name I say be silent, demon! This place is sealed against you. Be gone from my house to your master's hall, and do not return!"

Her words hung on the frantic air an instant, then the glass doors exploded, firing shards like diamonds out into the garden. The book slipped from her hands, popping open as it bounced to a page filled with dark symbols incised in muddy inks. She looked down to see them melt and flee away, all but for a few that swam together, merged into a shape almost catlike that leapt away. Yes, a golden cat not quite substantial, bumping its silken head under her hand. Placidly, it stopped, and seemed almost to blink, waiting.

"And as for you," said Donovan.

THANK YOU, MY LORD, MY LADY!

It was one spell too many for Susan. Her head swam, and her knees gave way. Donovan reached her just before her head could touch the floor. Neither of them noticed, not consciously, the golden streak that darted away from the book, hopped up on the settee and thence into a window where it stopped to wash its paws.

Breathing hard, Ned pulled Susan into his arms, his beloved, his betrothed, whispering all manner of foolishness at her until she stirred and spoke.

"Edward Donovan, what on earth are you doing?"

"Delighting in your brilliance and your admirable strength, of course," he said, "Susannah Adele Pickering, who is soon to be my wife."

She blinked owlishly, but raised no objection, so he helped her to the sofa. Solemnly, he touched straight the glasses on her nose, while she twisted up her hair.

In a minute the questions would start. There would be time for answers later. Right now . . .

"Miss Pickering," said Donovan artlessly. "I believe that was the gong for tea?"

"Indeed, Mr Donovan. I believe it was." Unsteady but determined, Susan let him lead her away.

The End

ENJOY AN EXCERPT FROM *THE DRAGON RING*, THE MAGICAL FIRST VOLUME OF THE HARPER ERRANT SERIES.

Iveston on the Moor, Devon, England

THE KING'S RAVEN SOARED UP OUT OF FAERIE, spiraling between banks of summer storm and into the sun over Dartmoor. The veils that cloak his world from ours fell together behind him like a crystalline song. Icy wedges of air streamed past the sharp eyes, poured across the stretching wings as he reached over the horizon for the moon's white disk. Then pivoting on a night-black wing tip, he turned and powered towards the ground, flipping barrel rolls for joy, because he could. Just as he flattened out to skim the granite-crowned tors, a glint of sapphire glittered at him from somewhere below.

Reluctant but obedient, he tumbled out of the sky over tiny Iveston village, stalled, and came to rest, wrapping hooked talons over the fence that defined the well-ordered yard of a country pub from the wild moor lands beyond. For a moment, he was a laughing young man sitting on the fence in black jeans and shirt. Then the elegant gentleman who had called him snapped an order, clearly expecting to be obeyed.

Vulgarly impertinent, the boy was the raven again. His head bobbed once, and again, in case his lord had missed the courtesy.

(He hadn't, and couldn't resist smiling.) Shouted a territorial caw, in case the ordinary *corvidae* in the neighborhood had missed his arrival. Then he sprang up with a noisy clap of wings to settle on the roof peak of the pub called Day's Star. On guard, eyes bright, he settled in.

Inside the lime-washed and serviceable Star, its dark interior redolent of time and beer, things were not so poetic. Well, not entirely. A pair of old men bent over a chess game in a corner under horse brasses and framed headlines from the Great War. Another, content to sit alone with his Kindle reader and a short whisky, took up the seat nearest the bar, occupied by his father and grandfather in their turns. Quiet enough, then, excepting the click of the e-reader paging, and the occasional muttered "Check!" There's a bit of poetry in all of that, maybe.

Mr Day, the landlord, added a metallic clank and thump to the mix, fitting a new keg in under the bar. But the sound that rang up to the sharp-eared Raven on the roof was none of these: less content, much younger, and utterly American.

"I said no, Peter, and I meant it! Just no!" Ben Harper had been reviewing galley proofs of the new book all day and had come down to the pub for a sandwich and a pint. "I should never have picked up," he muttered.

"What's that, eh?" said his agent.

Ben sighed and let the other man go on. It was an agent's job to keep the magic going, and wild ideas that worked were Peter's specialty, yes. He was the one who had turned Ben's knack for efficiency and clear thinking from a cottage industry into a career. So he was grateful. Really. The man earned his percentage, but there were limits. There had to be!

Ben drained his pint and gave up.

"Peter, stop. Could you stop? I said, no castles. No US locations. Maybe next year."

"Just let me finish, mate! This is brilliant! You'll love this."

Ben set the cell phone gently on the table and raised his empty glass and a meaningful look to Mr Day, who nodded back.

"Sorry? Sorry, Peter, you're breaking up!" Ben shouted, and with guilty satisfaction, tapped the call closed. Most of Dartmoor didn't even get cell service. Calls got dropped here all the time. It could be minutes before Peter noticed and rang back. A few blessed minutes, Ben thought. Maybe longer.

A fresh pint of Day's Best Bitter appeared in front of him, tiny bubbles rising through the gold to a thin, creamy head. When a second one materialized next to it, he looked up again, confused.

A quick flare of sunlight flooded the window over Ben's head, rendering his benefactor more or less invisible.

"Hope you don't mind."

The pleasant voice might have come out of the air, or from another world, there was no way to tell. Then a cloud, or something, softened the light again, and the comfortable shadows returned. The voice became a shape, then a man, and a whole new problem. Harper blinked and dropped his glasses back down to his nose.

Wary, he tipped his thanks with the fresh pint. "I don't usually accept drinks from strange men."

It was part of Ben's nature to notice, catalog, file, and he did it now without thinking. The tall, lordly type in beautifully tailored jacket and a silk shirt of pale but uncertain color smiled at him, then dragged up a chair and sat down opposite. Black hair curled loosely on the man's shoulders framing a sharp-featured face. Celtic, perhaps, or more exotic than that. Eurasian, maybe. High cheekbones touched with warmth, fine features, dark eyes so deeply blue they matched the sapphire that winked in one slightly pointed ear. A tendril of smoke spun up from the cigarette he held cupped between long manicured fingers.

Ben shot a questioning look back towards the bar; Mr Day just shrugged.

"Aubrey." The accent was plummy and posh, like the manner, if perhaps just a touch foreign. Not from around here, no. "Aubrey King."

"I'm sorry—Oberon? Not a name you hear a lot."

A cloud slipped off the sun again, and a stray sunbeam highlighted the planes of the face. He might almost have been posing for a magazine. Or an album cover. Ben suspected the guy was aware of the effect he created.

The fellow lifted one sable eyebrow, chuckled lightly as if he heard that all the time, the picture of aristocratic ease. The old wooden chair didn't even creak when he settled back in it.

"Aubrey," he corrected. Aubrey took a deliberate drag on the cigarette, then carefully let it out over his shoulder. "Been following your career, Ben Harper. Have a proposition for you."

Ben rolled his eyes, manners collapsing altogether. "Oh, of course you do."

Conversations that started like this invariably involved a unique opportunity he didn't need and couldn't afford. For the sake of distraction, he nodded at the cigarette. "Y'know, you can't smoke in here."

"Ah!" said Aubrey, his glance flickering to the cigarette with a grace note of surprise that might even have been genuine. "Quite right. Old habits."

He made a show of pinching out the cherry, then folding the stub into his palm. With a gesture like a stage magician, he fanned open the fingers again and it was gone.

"My 7-year-old can pull a quarter out of your ear."

We know the Sparrow! Yes, we do!

Listen!

Silly human!

What the hell? Tiny voices like a pack of munchkins were giggling somewhere, maybe under the window behind him, or just outside the door that stood open to the car park.

"Pfft," said the guy, Aubrey. "Pixies."

"Yeah, okay," Ben said. "Or kids." But he did wonder if the school had let out already. He had to pick up his son today.

In fact, he thought, it was probably time to go. Yeah, he should go. He tipped back his glass for a last appreciative swallow, and set it down a bit harder than he intended. By all rights it should have sloshed beer over the rim, but it didn't.

He stared at the glass for a second, then stood up. "Sorry. I really have to go." Feeling churlish but in suddenly desperate need of open air, he flung himself away from the table.

An enigmatic smile hovered around his lordship's mouth as the dark eyes tracked the American. "I think you'll find it's not the kind of proposition you expect."

"It never is, mate. But whatever it is, I really don't have the time," Ben said over his shoulder, and added with the barest courtesy, "Thanks for the beer."

He ducked under the low doorway to emerge, striding out across the pub's postage stamp front garden. Before his eyes had even finished adjusting to the light, the clouds parted then closed an instant later. Dazzled, running shoes skidding on the wet grass, Ben drew up short before he could slam into a picnic table still beaded with rain.

Vision cleared, and there was Aubrey.

He stared, then flung a look back over his shoulder towards the doorway he'd just come through. The man still appeared to be sitting at the table, calmly sipping his beer.

Again he looked to the rail fence where Aubrey couldn't possibly be but manifestly was. The double-take might have been comical if it weren't so bloody impossible. Ben pushed his wire-rimmed glasses up his nose with one finger. Who was this guy?

"Okay," he said carefully, backing away from the table, and the stranger. "Nice trick. I'm sure your idea is utterly unique, won't cost me a thing, and will make me rich."

A thin smile lifted Aubrey King's eyes, but he just put his hands in his pockets, shifted his weight, and said nothing.

"But could you just, y'know, call my agent, okay? He vets brilliant ideas all day long."

Like a criminal seeking sanctuary, Ben was edging backwards toward the pleasant darkness of the Star. He had taken no more than a few steps when a huge bird dived out of nowhere with a harsh cry, cutting the space between the two men. Ben stumbled back as a night-black wing tip nearly clipped his nose.

"Hey!"

The bird banked, traced a figure-eight around Aubrey, and soared back up to the roof. It snapped its beak and trained its black eye on the American, then gave a throaty croak, as if having the final word.

There was that childish giggling again.

"Aw, come on!"

Ben stared around, a little frantically. Still no children. Behind him, the figure with the beer had gone. And Aubrey just stood there by the front gate, calmly looking back at him. There was something else about the guy, despite the casual pose, that Ben couldn't quite put a name to. An air of...what?

Ben shivered slightly, then sighed again. If this was what stress was doing to him even before the new series started shooting, he was in serious trouble.

"Damn," he breathed.

And then he started to laugh—at himself, at the day, at life. Shaking his head, he gave up and walked back across the grass with a rueful smile. As he put out his hand, his gaze for the first time rose to meet Aubrey's long blue eyes, dark and strange as the sea.

"Look, I don't know what's going on."

"Going on?" said Aubrey.

Ben said, "Sorry," and realized he meant it. "I'm listening. What can I do for you?"

Aubrey put his hand in Ben's, accepting the apology with a nod.

"It's going to take some explaining," he said. "And some time. Ah! I know, that word again. But time is not really the problem, Ben. At least, not in the way you think."

"Oh, now you're just being mysterious."

The aristocratic smirk again. "You did leave a pint of perfectly good beer on the table. Shall we go in?"

Pushing a fringe of sandy hair back out of his eyes, Ben looked at the man, really looked at him. "Are you glowing?"

Well, he was. Not in any vulgar, glittery way but a glow indeed—an aura maybe—pale in the watery, unreliable light.

"Am I?"

That eyebrow lifted again with amusement and something else Ben couldn't guess at.

When the clouds moved again, it was gone. "Hmm, maybe not."

Stress, Ben thought. And sunlight bouncing into his eyes. English springs are notorious for bright intervals of sun and shadow. And technically, it was still spring for another week or so. If the yard seemed perceptibly darker, that would be the trailing edge of the earlier storm slipping by on its way to Surrey.

"Curious," Aubrey said. "So. Drinks?"

Time appeared to be the recurring theme of a day growing steadily more odd.

"It's— I don't know." Ben checked his watch, then turned to look down the street toward the sixteenth century clock tower and past it to Iveston School. "Damn it! I've got to get my son from school. Would you mind—?"

"May I walk with you?" Aubrey King gestured with grace.

"Uhm, okay."

Compartmentalizing out of habit, and because he saw no other choice, Ben set the weirdness aside and crunched down the driveway and into the road, with the tall, fae gentleman strolling easily at his left hand.

The half-timbered pile that was the Star (EST. 1621) sprawled at one end of the village. The school in serviceable red brick lay, wisely, at the other. As Iveston was one of Devon's smaller villages, the two ends were not all that far apart, with little more than the vicarage and the consecrated breadth of St Michael's church (EST. 1528) between them. As they passed the ancient lychgate leading to the graveyard, Ben felt more than heard the other man take a step back, then cut behind him with a rhythm almost like a dance step, to walk on the other, sunnier side of the street. The green smell of the moor washed over them as he moved, and a light scent of violets.

"Issues with the Church?" Ben asked with a curious grin.

"In a manner of speaking," the other man said, without elaborating. A raven, probably not the same one, called from somewhere. "Indeed," he added obscurely, smiling.

They walked on with Ben expecting a hard sales pitch at any moment. Instead, the man was humming a clever little tune he'd never heard before.

"Who are you?" said Ben suddenly. "Really?"

Aubrey's face lit up, as if he had been waiting for this question, then appeared to reconsider. Finally he shrugged and said slowly, "What if I told you I was Oberon, king of Faerie?"

Ben snorted. "I'd look around for hidden cameras. Or the men in the white coats."

"Yes, I suppose you would. Still, it might be true. This is Dartmoor, the heart of England's magick, and there are stories. The fae, it's well known, cannot lie."

"So they say," Ben allowed. "But come on, who are you? What are you? Reporter? Rock star? I know, super hero. Is this your secret identity?"

That made Aubrey laugh out loud. "I knew I liked you," he said without answering. When they finally stepped onto the sidewalk in front of the low wall that protected the school from the street, he faced the American soberly.

"The real question, Ben Harper, is who are you? An efficiency expert who has no time? A musician who never plays? An actor of more than ordinary charm who's content to be a TV star writing housekeeping manuals?"

"Hey!"

The voice was light, almost mocking, but the expression was serious. "What other gifts are you neglecting? Don't you wonder?"

Ben pushed his glasses up again. It's not like he hadn't been asking himself those very questions lately. Lately, and for a while, in fact. But having someone else fling his doubts in his face, doubts he'd barely begun to share with his wife, was something else again.

"Hey," he repeated, and felt stupid when he did. Not exactly a devastating comeback for the man's too-accurate assessment. A few yards away, the clock on the school wall ticked over another loud minute before Ben said, annoyed: "So, what is this, a rescue? Some kind of intervention? Are you the ghost of Christmas Yet to Come? Who put you up to this?"

His new friend, if that's what he was, stiffened slightly. So much for his more than ordinary charm. It sounded insulting even to Ben.

Those pixies, or small children, were laughing at him again or maybe it was the wind in the oak tree just over the way.

"Okay," Ben said as the strained silence lengthened. "Just tell me what's going on."

Now the man did crack a smile. "You're collecting your child from school, I thought. What's his name again?"

The awkwardness shifted.

"Uh, Sparrow. He's called Sparrow."

Ben pushed open the chain link gate to join the cluster of waiting parents applying their x-ray vision to the smoked glass doors for the first glimpse of their kids. Alas, parental super powers were on the fritz today. All anyone could see were their own fun-house reflections.

Aubrey considerately stayed behind, leaning his back against the wall, paying attention to the village instead of making the other grown-ups nervous. Well, maybe that was the motivation, but when Ben looked back he had that feeling again, of some kind of power restrained and contained. For all the relaxed elegance, the man stood like a soldier on guard, scanning for trouble. Who was this guy?

Abruptly, the flat buzz of the school bell jangled the country quiet, and the question slipped away. In seconds the tiniest children burst shrieking through the double doors in a bobbing river of robin's egg blue, and slammed into parental knees. Before they'd quite cleared the hallway, a half-dozen 7- and 8-year-olds came barreling through, their gap-toothed smiles as sunny as summer days.

Next week—no, tomorrow, Ben realized—was the last day of term. No wonder they looked so especially cheerful. They'd be free, and two weeks later he'd be back at his London desk, living on fast food and coffee, the willing architect of his own depression. Willing, mind you. Which brought him back to Aubrey King and the favor that hadn't yet been asked. King of the faeries, oh yeah. Still, there was something.

Where the hell was Sparrow?

A light glimmered behind the tinted doors, a child skipping, tow head bobbing like the bird that had given him his nickname. You'd never know, most of the time, how delicate he really was. As he pressed through the doors, cheerful but paler than usual under the sunny hair, Ben noted with worry the signs of strain on the kid's face. Something had happened—an asthma attack? How severe? The medication usually worked, but now and then Sparrow pushed himself too hard to keep up with the other kids. Things happened; Ben made the effort to stay cool.

The teacher was bringing him out, one hand on the slender shoulder as if trying to keep him from floating away.

"Daddy!" Sparrow started to break away but the restraining hand caught him back. He squirmed while Daddy exchanged a few words with Teacher about chronic illness and activity levels. Daddy took his hand.

Might be worse, the grown-ups agreed. Might still be living in Los Angeles.

Impatient, Sparrow squiggled, bounced, and danced, still tethered to Daddy but distracted by everything, humming some little hum that wasn't quite a song. Unless it was. The pixies had been singing with him at lunchtime today, before the asthma started up, and now he heard the tune again, all twisty and strange. Two or three of the pixie folk were pulling at him, dragging at his shoelaces, and babbling in their tiny voices. One of them squeaked and pointed, until he looked up.

A wee man just about the size and shape of a garden gnome stood on the wall wearing a curious coat of leather and leaves, with a red feather in his pointed cap like a safety flag. Sparrow giggled, as he always did, for the wee man's nose was so long and curved down that it almost touched his chin, and his chin was so long and curved up that it almost touched his nose. They'd met before. And he was chatting familiarly with a tall, dark haired man wearing a golden crown and a sober expression.

The man said something. The wee man roared with laughter. It hopped on one foot three times, spun around, and vanished with a *pop!* Sparrow gasped. The kingly man looked down and met the child's awed gaze.

Sparrow knew better than to talk to big strangers, even faerie ones, so he whipped back around at once, suddenly shy, and tightened his grip on Daddy's hand. He had meant to give a loud, impatient sigh, but forgot.

Finally, Miss Martin went away, and it was time to go.

"How now, gentle knight," said Ben, giving the boy his complete attention—finally. "Your charger awaits. Will ye ride?"

"Good my lord, so shall I," Sparrow cried, because he was his father's son.

❧

Continue the adventure in paperback or e-book at amazon.com, Smashwords.com, and other online booksellers

About the Author

Maggie Secara started out wanting to be an archaeologist. Then a reporter, then an international spy, a poet, an opera singer, a novelist, a historian. She ended up being a bit of each, earning a Masters degree in English and becoming involved with historical costume and improvisational theatre. When all those passions came together at once, she decided to be a novelist again, and so she did. Her short fiction has appeared in a variety of publications, including New Realm and Unsung Stories magazines. She is currently working on a collection of her short fiction.

Maggie lives in Los Angeles, California, with one adoring husband, two goofy cats, and half a million English words to toy with.

You can find Maggie in all these entertaining places:

Facebook   facebook.com/groups/maggiesworlds
Twitter   twitter.com/MaggiRos
Tumblr   maggie-secara.tumblr.com/
Pinterest pinterest.com/maggiros/
Goodreads.com/author/show/1632490.Maggie_Secara

For historical backgrounds, concept art, music videos, free stories, and coming attractions, or to leave comments for Maggie, please visit the website at www.maggiesecara.com

If you enjoyed this book, please consider leaving a review to assist other readers in their choices.

www.ingramcontent.com/pod-product-compliance
Lightning Source LLC
Chambersburg PA
CBHW070639130626
46555CB00006B/2617